JOURNEY OF DEATH

JOURNEY OF DEATH

by

John Dyson

Dales Large Print Books
Long Preston, North Yorkshire,
BD23 4ND, England.

British Library Cataloguing in Publication Data.

Dyson, John
    Journey of death.

    A catalogue record of this book is
    available from the British Library

    ISBN   1-84262-182-3 pbk

First published in Great Britain 2001 by Robert Hale Limited

Copyright © John Dyson 2001

Cover illustration © Faba by arrangement with
Norma Editorial

The right of John Dyson to be identified as the author of this
work has been asserted by him in accordance with the
Copyright, Designs and Patents Act, 1988

Published in Large Print 2002 by arrangement with
Robert Hale Limited

Dales Large Print is an imprint of Library Magna Books Ltd.

Printed and bound in Great Britain by
T.J. (International) Ltd., Cornwall, PL28 8RW

One

There's a big difference between killing a man in cold blood, and killing a man in hot blood. What I would term cold-blooded killing happened in the Big War when we defended our land from a horde of lousy Yankees, shooting from the barricades at men we never knew by name. Again, my carbine has been employed plenty after the war working as a cowhand on ranches in my native New Mexico, repelling raiders, both Mex and Mescaleros, who tried to run off the stock. In both cases I killed in a strangely detached kind of way, the killings sanctioned by the laws of war or of the range. But until I strolled, or maybe staggered, through the gates of the Broken Back ranch I had never killed hot-bloodedly. What I'm talking about is killing somebody up close, somebody who claims to be a friend, who had helped me, killing him spurred by anger, envy and lust. And knowing that, if I am apprehended, the penalty is to have the life choked out of me, strung high, my boots kicking air.

'Yeah, what yo wan', *hombre?*' A mean-looking varmint in a black hat, black clothes, with a down-turned vee of heavy moustache, was scowling down the sights of a twelve-gauge shotgun. 'You lookin' for work?'

'Maybe.'

That afternoon I was no hot-blooded murderer, nor wanted to be. The sweat was pouring from me as I hefted my saddle, soogans, Winchester carbine, near-empty wooden canteen, the bridle of my dead bronc hooked around my neck, a guitar slung across my back, and two Colt Lightnings stuck in the holsters of a double gunbelt of brass slugs. Without a horse a man can feel mighty weighed down.

'What you mean, maybe?'

'I mean' – my lips were so dry I could hardly speak – 'I might be. Depends.'

It was hot, damned hot, and I must have been walking for two hours, ten or twelve miles, through one of the most desolate areas in the United States. One of the most dangerous, too. In fact, as I climbed the trail up along the copper-streaked cliff-side of the Tiwa mountain I had been more than surprised and relieved to see the sign, with its skull of a longhorn perched on top, and the adobe and log ranch buildings set back not far off the road.

'Depends on what?' He was thickset and middle aged, sat on horseback, as iron-nerved as any man who ever aimed a double-barrel at a fellow man. 'Hey, speak up.'

My clothes were clinging to me, my long johns, jeans and batwing chaps making it hard work walking. That's to say nothing of my boots. Oh, those high-heeled boots! They weren't made for walking. And through a hole in one of my socks I'd already got a dandy blister on my heel.

'That depends on whether I can make it to that tank.' I had spotted a wide, low-walled well in the dusty yard at which two Mexican women were slapping clothes. 'Right now all I need's some of that water.'

He turned his big horse and followed me as I teetered in on my red-hot soles, dumped my heavy load, eased my aching shoulders, and doffed my straw sombrero at the Mex washerwomen, both as skinny and ugly as rats.

'Howdy, *muchachas.*'

I fell forward dunking my head and shoulders in the pool not caring that the murky fluid did taste like dirty socks, if not worse.

In those drought-dry parts a man will drink anything that's wet.

'OK, mister, you've had your drink. You want a job or not?' The shotgun was turning nasty. 'If not, fill your canteen and on your way.'

'Sure,' I gasped, flicking my long black hair out of my eyes in a flurry of rainbow-hued droplets. 'What's the big hurry?'

'In these parts,' he growled, 'we don't like strangers hanging about.'

'Maybe,' I said, 'you could sell me a horse?'

'I dunno about that.'

'Harry,' a voice called. 'What's the problem?'

Harry turned and drawled, 'No problem, boss.'

'Come in.' A floridly fat man was sat beneath a wattle canopy on the porch of what I took to be the main ranch house although it was a tad tumbledown. He beckoned to us with a finger. 'Come here.'

I followed the surly shotgun over to him and was glad of the shade after trudging through the midday heat with that load on my back. Without being invited I sank on to a roughly carpentered chair and leaned my elbow on his table, wiping my bandanna

10

across my damp forehead.

'Whoo! Am I glad to be rid of that burden. I lost my horse.'

'That was careless of you.'

The fat man, wearing a gaudy, billowing shirt over his pants, had surprisingly delicate facial features almost swamped by his double chins and reams of flesh. He had the nose of an aristocrat and his little pink mouth was smiling.

'Where did you lose it?'

'What happened is she broke her foreleg. I had to shoot her. You got a bronc you can sell me cheap? I got ten dollars to spare.'

The shotgun laughed. 'Last of the big spenders. We don't have no horses to spare at that price.'

'That's true. We're short of stock, ourselves.' The fat man was sipping at a flute of white wine, the bottle on the table half-empty, and had obviously just finished an ample lunch. He picked out an olive from the remains of a salad, slowly chewed it and spat out the pit. 'The Messys ran most of ourn off.'

'The Mescaleros? I thought they were on the reservation.'

'Some are,' the shotgun put in. 'Some ain't.'

It was not good news to me, not if I had to go on, on foot, alone. If the Mescaleros had started raiding again I could be walking out towards certain death, but, in retrospect, I wished I'd taken my chances of an arrow in the back rather than stay at the Broken Back ranch.

'Where you from, son?' The large, flabby dude pushed across a flask of water and a plate of toasted bread-chunks. 'Help yourself.'

'I been working for Uncle John down on the Pecos.'

'Uncle' John was, of course, not my uncle, but John Chisum, the big cattle baron of the Territory. By comparison this place appeared to be a hole-in-the-wall outfit. Whatever land they owned must be set back off the trail up in the mountains. The grass would be poor, the terrain difficult and dangerous. When I left the Pecos I had headed up the Rio Hondo from the Chisum ranch passing through Lincoln and pausing awhile in White Oaks. My intention was to reach Socorro on the Rio Grande. From there maybe I would go north to Albuquerque and Santa Fe.

'Why leave Chisum?'

'Why not?' I looked enviously at his bottle

of *vino,* which the greedy pig hadn't offered me. Still, dry toast and water was probably more thirst-quenching. So, I took a drink and crunched toast. 'I'm just a saddle bum. I don't stay no place long. I like to see what's over the horizon.'

The fat man laughed. 'If you're heading for Socorro you got a long walk. About fifty miles, eh, Harry? Easy enough on horse-back, but I pity *you.*'

'I can do it.' I met his pale, red-rimmed eyes. He wafted perfume. There was something unhealthy about him. His silky hair was slicked back and there was a sickly smell of bay rum. 'I guess I'll do another ten miles tonight and camp out.'

All I'd have to fear were the fangs of some night-prowling sidewinder that don't have the courtesy to give a rattle before they strike. The Mescaleros you only had to worry about at dawn. 'I'll do the rest tomorrow.'

'What's your hurry?' The big boss gave his twisty little smile and bit the tip from a fat green Havana, spitting it away. The shotgun struck a match, somewhat hurriedly, and lit up for him. He sucked and puffed his cheeks like bellows before letting the blue smoke trickle out. 'Why not work for me?'

13

'What doing?' I had noticed there was some kind of mining operation going on where the red cliffs were being quarried not far from the dwellings. 'I ain't a pick-and-shovel man.'

'Copper? That's just a sideline. You carry guns so you doubtless know how to use them. I need protection for my herd. We're short of men. We had two fatalities but don't let that worry you.'

'I'm not worried. I'm just not interested, that's all. I've had enough of poking cows for a while.' I got to my feet. 'So, I guess I'll be on my way.'

The fat man seemed unperturbed as he lounged back on his rocker and smoked his cigar. 'Twenty a month all found's no good to you?'

'Twenty a month? For fighting Messys? That's chicken-feed.' Anyway, I had dreams of using my undoubted skill at cards, a certain sleight of hand, to support myself in a more civilized way in the saloons of Santa Fe, not be stuck out in the wilds of these 6,000 feet high mountains surrounded by hostile savages, breaking my butt riding a bronc all day. Admittedly, I hadn't done too well in the saloon at White Oaks and lost most of my grubstake, but my luck should soon change. 'Thanks for the offer...'

The screen door of the ranch door opened and a young woman stepped out, a tray in her hand. She had shiny blonde hair, assisted, I imagined, by that stuff the whores use, what is it, peroxide? And her face was made up like one, her pert nose powdered, her lips rouged. She stood looking out over the valley to the blue-shadowed mountain wall as the sun began its fall, as if lost in thought. But perhaps it was to give me a chance to admire her curves. Her tight-fitting, expensive white blouse and black skirt clung in all the right places. And when she turned to give me the full blast of her personality her eyes sparkled, sexily, and her lower lip jutted as defiantly as her breasts. To tell the truth, she made me go weak at the knees!

'So,' she drawled. 'We got company?'

'He's just leaving,' the fat man snapped.

Suddenly I had changed my mind. 'Aw, I dunno,' I stuttered. 'Maybe if you could up it to thirty a month, same as Chisum pays?'

'Twenty-five.'

'OK, but only for a month or so. Just as soon as I get myself a decent mount' – I locked my eyes with hers – 'then I'll be on my way.'

15

The large man laughed in his tinkly way. 'Suit yourself. Maybe you won't want to leave when you get to know us.'

'No' – I looked at her again and she gave a slight smile – 'maybe I won't.'

'What's your handle?'

'Angel Alvorado.'

'You a Mexican?'

'On my father's side. My mother was a Texas gal. Nope, I ain't Mex, I'm a citizen of the good ol' US of A. Why?'

'No reason.' The fat one offered a pudgy damp paw. 'When I saw the guitar I imagined you might be a travelling *mariachi*.'

'Nope. I just like a little music when I'm camping out by my lonesome fire.'

'Good. I like you. You've got soul. My name's Alexandre Quiros.' He let go of my hand. 'This is a land of mixed races. I am partly French. Would you believe I once had a hundred slaves on my estates in Louisiana? All set free after the War, my land taken from me, the crippling taxes ... what Robespierre began the Yankee government completed: the downfall of my noble line. 'This' – he waved his cigar – 'is all I have left. It is my new start in life.'

The blonde started clearing the lunch

16

plates. She emptied the bottle into his glass without a word, put the bottle on her tray and, on sandalled feet, returned to the house. I watched the sway of her hips beneath the bell-shaped skirt, the neat way she raised a knee to balance the tray as she opened the screen door.

'We've all had to suffer, I guess,' I muttered.

'Yes, but maybe, Angel, you are going to be our Angel of Light, harbinger of our changed fortunes.'

The flowery way the fat man spoke, and smiled lingeringly at me, I wondered for moments if he might be one of those weird guys, you know, that like other men. But, what the hell! Live and let live, I say. Or I did, at that moment in time.

'Harry will show you the bunkhouse,' Quiros said, dismissing me. 'You start work tomorrow at five a.m.'

'Who's the dame?' I asked, as I was led away.

'Belle? She's his wife. And if I were you I'd forget her, mister, unless you want trouble. Don't be fooled by Mr Quiros's manner. He's a hard man to cross.'

Forget her? How could I forget her? As I lay on my back in the musty bunkhouse

17

easing my blistered feet she was all I could think about. I knew I had to have her.

It wasn't the Angel of Light he should have called me, I thought afterwards. It was the Angel of Death.

Two

They were a rough-looking bunch who shambled into the bunkhouse that night. Ramrodder of the cowboys was Charley Bowdler, a mean, slit-eyed cuss, moustachios dangling to under his chin, and wearing range leathers, slung with iron. Alongside him came three shabby 'pokes, two just corn-sucking kids, the other a hard bitten and melancholy older man, Dan Coughlan. The miners were a dusty, nondescript collection, three of them Mexicans, the fourth another worn-out old guy, Abe Klasner, who all shuffled in after dusk, like convicts on a chain gang. The cowboys were typically high-spirited, boastful and blasphemous. But the miners seemed somehow secretive and cowed.

'You wouldn't catch me bent double down a dark hole with a pick and shovel,' I opined. 'I bet you guys ain't seen daylight in days. How much he pay you?'

'Not much,' one of the Mexicans hissed. 'But iss enough. Honest work hard to find thiss hard times.'

It was true. The south was in ruins after the War. Ex-soldiers and hard men had drifted into the West, most expert with guns and accustomed to indiscriminate killing. It was difficult for an ordinary man to settle and go straight. The honest ranchers were plagued by rustlers. Even Uncle John Chisum had had to move some of his vast herds back to the Texas Panhandle as the Lincoln County War blazed back and forth. That was one reason why I had packed in my job and headed higher up the Hondo valley. Why should I put my life on the firing line to protect a rich man's cattle for the small change us cowboys were paid?

'I tried my hand digging for gold at White Oaks. That's supposed to be the new bonanza town,' I told my buddy in the next bunk, who introduced himself as Jesus Guttierez. 'But I didn't have no luck. So, what are you bringing up here – copper?'

'*Si.*' Jesus showed the whites of his eyes as he rolled them towards the three other miners, who stared at him, strangely. 'Just copper.'

'What the hell good is that to anybody?'

The young Latino shrugged. 'Monsieur Quiros, he ship it down the Rio Grande to

Mesilla. Copper ees much in demand for bullet-casings.'

'You don't say? Well, I wouldn't work down a black hole for all the gold in China – if they got any – I like to be out under the blue sky riding free.'

So saying, I picked up my guitar and strummed a few chords, practising my fingering for, like with the revolver, it's daily practice that makes perfect. They pricked up their ears for the rippling music reminded them of good times in Old Mexico, and started called out requests.

A fast and furious bullring *pasa doble* had them enthralled, but a guy can't keep that up all night. I sang along to the more dolorus lament *'La Señorita de Minha Terra,'* and laid the instrument aside. That, of course, set them wailing for more.

'You know one thing I can't understand,' I told them, as I accepted a rolled cigarette, 'is why all you people who love music so much don't learn to play the damn guitar yourselves? You think I'm here to entertain you for free? Anybody wants to hear more they gonna have to pay me ten cents a tune.'

'Hi-yagh!' Charley Bowdler gave a whoop of glee. 'Listen to that mercenary bastard! That's how to shut up them miserly greasers. You tell 'em, cowboy.'

The mining fraternity down my end of the bunkhouse didn't argue. They just groaned and sighed, muttered their prayers and faded off into sleep. They had to be up at five a.m. and back down their mine. And, come to think of it, I had to be out on the range.

Charley picked me out a knock-kneed mustang from the corral. He fitted in the cruel spade bit that held the tongue hard down and prevented him getting the bit between his teeth. He had a hard mouth from being badly handled but it was an efficient brake. The scars along his sides showed that to accelerate a man had to spur him hard. The poor critter was just a ranch tool. When he was worn out he would be shot and left for the coyotes. But he would have to do for it was true that they didn't have much in the way of horseflesh.

'The boss says we're gonna have ta rustle up some more hosses.' Charley pulled his battered hat, its front brim bent back, hard down over his long greasy hair. 'But first we're gonna check the cattle.'

I didn't much like the sound of that 'rustle up'. My plan had been to go straight, not cross the line.

'If I wanted to be a rustler I'd go into it on my own account, not for the lousy few bucks Quiros is paying me.'

'You hear that, boys? Mistuh Quiros has hired a chicken.' Charley grinned and slapped my shoulder as one of the young hicks started crowing like a hen, taunting me. 'Doncha worry, Angel. There'll be cash in it for us.'

Now, I was well aware that rounding up horses or cattle that bore another man's brand was a popular diversion in New Mexico Territory and not regarded as a serious crime. But a cowboy who was caught red-handed could be shot or made to kick the clouds and I was not happy about this.

'Look at his face,' Shoot Stevens, the chicken-cackler, jeered. 'He's sceered he's got inta bad company.'

I whipped out my left-hand double-action Lightning .38 and aimed it at him. 'One more crack outa you, asshole, an' you'll be shittin' your pants before dying.'

Shoot looked surprised and scared, raising his hands. 'Hey, what's wrong? I'm only joking.'

I held him in my sights for a few seconds,

aimed between his eyes, lowered the revolver and spun it backwards into its holster, as the others burst into laughter.

'Shoot, Shoot, you'd better learn to shoot,' Charley cackled, 'while this *hombre*'s with us.' He hauled his mount around and spurred it away up a trail into the mountains. 'Come on.'

We rode for miles as the sun climbed high into the sky, and we climbed into the Sierra Blanca range. We passed plenty of bunches of cattle with the Broken Back brand. At noon we reached a natural horseshoe-shaped hole in the mountainside, fed by a clear spring, inside which some scrawny longhorns and their calves bawled aimlessly. The entranceway was barred by a few poles and rocks.

'These are a few we found t'other day,' Charley said, as he dismounted. 'There's more where they come from.'

The boys started putting the coffee-can on a rock fireplace and getting a blaze going, young Shoot producing a branding-iron which he set to heat in the flames. I loosened my mustang's cinch and let him graze.

'Just where would that be?' I asked, eyeing the longhorns' Barbed Y branch. 'Ain't that

24

Pete Rudulph's stock?'

'Aw, he won't miss a few. All we gotta do is ride up the western side of the caprock.' Charley pointed a gloved finger towards Rudulph's land. 'We'll round up a few drifting strays. We gotta work fast 'fore his cowboys start their round-up. We'll sell 'em down at White Oaks. The miners'll pay twelve dollars a head.'

'The gov'ment contractors at Fort Stanton'll pay double that,' one of my other young companions, named Windy Ridge, put in. 'Why don't we herd 'em there?'

'Because it's another twenty-five miles an' it's easier to get to White Oaks,' Charley snapped. 'Who's running this outfit?'

'Yeah, but double your money,' our fourth cowpoke, Dan Couglan, croaked. 'Ain't it worth it for that?'

'Hell, do I have to do all the thinkin'? We're not the greatest brand artists, an' the military can git mighty suspicious. Those hungry miners down at White Oaks will buy anything that's goin'.' Charley shook his head with dismay. 'There's also the possibility of running into Rudulph and his boys. We wanna git these off our hands as fast as we can.'

I have to say, although Charley spoke

sense, I was worried. I had no great wish to become some ne'er-do-well rustler with a price on my head. I had a hankering to become somebody in this world. And I knew who I wanted to become that somebody with: Belle. But, was it possible she would be interested, in spite of her flirtatious glances, in some down-at-heel saddle-bum with no more than a few cents in his pocket? Was it likely she would leave her rich husband, grossly fat as he was, for me? I needed a few dollars in my wallet if I planned to move on.

So, all I asked was, as I squatted down and sucked at a tin cup of scalding black coffee, 'How about Quiros?'

'What Quiros don't know he don't miss.' Charley winked at me. 'He's got enough cows to keep him happy.'

'Yeah,' Shoot giggled. 'An' how about that blonde one of his? I bet she gives him a buzz.'

I tossed my coffee dregs into the fire, moving away, not wishing to listen to Shoot's obscenities about what that beautiful young woman might be doing that very moment in the fat man's bed. Their words splattered about me. They were talking about the woman I loved. I turned to them in a pent-up fury and shouted, 'Why don't you shut up?'

They were silent a few moments. Then Charley whistled and cooed, 'Hey, I figure he's got the hots for Belle.'

Their cackling laughter was making my blood boil. I grabbed my lariat, strode over to a bunch of cattle and roped a calf as he tried to escape. I pulled him to me and flung him down on his side, tying his back-hoofs and dragging him to the fire as he cried, piteously. 'Hey,' I said. 'Ain't it time we got some work done? Get your iron.'

The calf bawled as his hide hissed and Shoot doctored the Barbed Y with the branding iron, turning it into a Forked Y. It was a bit of a bodged job and really needed to be allowed to grow in. 'Pretty obvious,' I muttered, 'but I guess it'll do. Come on, let's get another one.'

After an hour's work most of the small bunch were roped and branded and the dust rose in a hot cloud smelling of burned hide.

'Right,' Charley cried. 'Let's go find some more. Tomorrow we'll trail 'em into White Oaks. We'll have us a time and be back by the end of the week.'

'What about Quiros?' I asked again. 'Won't he wonder where we've gotten to?'

'What's the matter, Angel?' Windy jeered. 'You in a hurry to get back and drool over his wife?'

'You can fergit her.' The hard-faced Charley swung into the saddle. 'You won't git nowhere. She flaunts herself at all the new boys. She's just a cock-teaser. Don't worry, there's plenty two-bit whores down at White Oaks.'

'Yeah,' I groaned, not too pleased. 'I been there before.'

Three

White Oaks was a new boom town that had sprung up overnight. The strike was nowhere as big a bonanza as at Virginia City, Idaho, or Alder Gulch, Montana, or even at Tombstone, Arizona, but it was big enough to attract starry-eyed miners, forever seeking the mother lode, to New Mexico. This narrow, mountain-girt valley out in the wilderness some forty-five miles by wagon road north-west of Lincoln, had suddenly become as busy as a hive of bees.

'Geed along there!' Charley cried, snaking his seven-foot bullwhip to crack over the backs of our stolen herd of seventy longhorns as they went plunging and tossing through the trail between the pitch-roofed cabins that sprawled up the sides of the valley on either side. 'OK,' he yelled at Shoot and Windy who were riding point. 'Slow 'em down.'

The rutted main drag we were in was sided by various ramshackle establishments such as Hairy Martha's Dairy, the Nan

King Chinese Laundry, Freund and Bro., Guns and Munitions, Kadinsky, Loans, Murphy's Meat Market, Joshua Dunn, Gold Dust Bought, all displaying false fronts painted with crude and apposite signs, such as a cow or a gun. There were also ten saloons and bawdy-houses, all, even in this early afternoon, vibrating with music, laughter and shrill female screams. There were hitched horses and wagons and folks milling to and fro. A teamster who had hauled a double wagon-load of whiskey and supplies up from Lincoln City was about to abandon his ten-mule team and head into the Claremont Hotel and Saloon.

'Hey, mister,' Shoot called. 'Can you park your rig across the street and corral our herd in?'

'What's in it for me?'

'Drinks on us once we sell this bunch.'

'Done.' The teamster cracked his whip and, with the customary cussing, manoeuvred his mules to block the street. 'You kin find me inside.'

We didn't need to waste much time finding a buyer. A small-time rancher wanted the calves to build up his herd and gave us nine dollars a head. The scarlet-faced butcher, Murphy, came running up and grabbed the rest at fifteen dollars each.

We left them to separate the calves from the cows and headed for the Claremont, leaping up on to the wooden sidewalk as Charley counted the cash.

'Thass about a hundred and thirty dollars each,' he said, swaggering into the saloon, spurs clanking on the plank floor, and dividing the spoils into five piles on the bar counter. We didn't argue about his arithmetic but tucked the greenbacks and gold coin into our pockets, as a bottle of whiskey and five tankards of beer came sliding along the bar.

'Howdy.' A couple of fellows I had known when I was grubbing for gold in the hills were standing at the bar and turned to join me. 'I thought you said you were heading for Santa Fe. Can't you bear to leave us?'

'My hoss broke her leg. I've taken a job up at the Broken Back outfit in the hills north of here. It's only temporary.'

'Looks to me,' one of them said, glancing at the yipping and yahooing Charley and the boys, 'you've gotten into bad company.'

'Aw, they're OK,' I mumbled.

'Don't that weird Frenchman run that place?'

'Yep, the fat guy. He's OK.'

'The one with the classy wife?'

'Belle? Yeah, I seen better.'

'He's got a mine shaft up there. What's he coming up with? Any sign of gold?'

'No, copper. At least, that's what I'm told.'

'Copper? What's he want to mine for copper for when there's gold in these hills?'

'Beats me. But he sells it for ammo casings. I guess it pays.'

'Yeah? Take care, Angel. Don't drink too much of that stuff.'

He could say that again. I knew as soon as this mob started on the hooch there'd be no stopping them until their pockets were empty. Not me. I was going to hang on to some of my loot, try to keep a clear head and put it to good use at the gambling tables.

Famous last words, as they say.

Two days later my pile of 130 dollars from selling the stolen cows was all but gone. Five months' wages to any ordinary cowboy. The two hicks, Shoot and Windy, looked jaded and worn after cavorting with every prairie nymph they could find in White Oaks. Charley and Dan were sick, sullen and looked like they'd got the staggers and shakes as they sat in a corner and tried to drink the town dry. As for me, well, I didn't feel much better. I sat in on roulette, monte and faro, even tried throwing dice along with a crowd of bums in a back alley, but the luck wasn't with me.

Now I'd gotten myself into a poker game that wasn't going at all my way. The gang of miners were keeping their cards close to their chests; one in particular, a big, beer-gutted, black-bearded bear giving me very suspicious glances. But I had to try to salvage some of my crooked earnings. It was time for a little twisting of Lady Luck's arm. I had kept my spare ace in my sleeve. I snaked it out into my palm and inserted it neatly into the pack as I shuffled, making sure it came my way.

The trick is to divert their attention and stay calm and straight-faced. It is a game of bluff, after all. Yes, I had a good hand. I could take them. I pushed my last dollar into the pot. Blackbeard watched me with one beady eye as we played.

'How about that, boys?' I drawled, as I spread my cards. 'Looks like my luck's in at last.'

'You cheating bastard.' The Big Bear was stumbling to his feet, his mouth an ugly grimace as he fumbled to draw the heavy percussion pistol from his belt. I tipped myself back, instinctively, falling against the wall. He fired and his lead shattered the woodwork above my head. I whipped out my right hand self-cocking Lightning and emptied three slugs in fast succession into his chest. Blood spilled as he cried out and rolled away across the floor. I stood and put another in the back of his hairy head to make sure of him. But he was dead. Dead as the dodo.

The crowd of miners looked uneasy in the silence as the black powder smoke billowed across the saloon. Some were groping at their guns. This could have been a sticky situation. But Charley was up, his carbine in his hands, Dan beside him.

'I wouldn't try anythang, gents,' Charley yelled. 'That was a fair fight.'

'Nope,' Shoot crooned from the top of the stairs as he leaned over the balustrade, a revolver in his hand, Windy beside him. 'We saw it all. The big fella went for him first.'

'I guess it was self-defence,' one of the miners sat opposite me agreed. 'But I ain't sure it weren't true what he said. If I was you, mister, I would take your lousy winnings and go. Bill had friends around. And this town don't need your kind.'

'My kind?' I said, but looking around at

Charley and his sidekicks, their guns aimed, I had a good idea what he meant: petty criminals, card-sharps, drunks, whore-mongers, and troublemakers. 'Sure,' I agreed, scooping in my ill-gotten winnings. 'I know when I ain't wanted. But this was a fair game. You be sure to tell the sheriff that iffen he asks.'

We all backed out of the saloon and went to look for our broncs in the livery.

'Time to be gittin' back, boys,' Charley hooted, slapping me on the back, proudly. 'Good shootin', Angel. We don't take that crap from nobody. You're one of us now.'

We saddled up and headed out of town and I must say I'd got the butterflies inside, both excited and scared. It was, after all, the first gunfight I'd had in public and I wasn't sure it was a good idea. The old adage crossed my mind: 'He who lives by the gun dies by the gun.' And I very much wanted to live.

'Hey,' young Windy Ridge called as we rode out. 'Look at 'em staring at us. Angel's quite a shootist. He's gonna make a name for himself.'

Four

A reputation as a gunslinger was something I didn't need, it occurred to me, as we rode back across country the way we had come. Guns had been part of my life since childhood and I had honed my skills as a sharpshooter in the War. But hadn't I seen my own father gunned down by a couple of desperadoes when he was sheriff of Silver City? Hadn't he warned me that if a man gained a name as a fast gun, especially if he had Mexican blood, sooner or later some young punk would come looking to prove himself faster? The shock of my first saloon gun-duel was still with me. I had killed a man for what? Forty-three dollars in a crooked card-game! Was that something to be proud of?

But the boys were in high spirits as we rode back. To them, to kill a man was a feather in their cap. Rather than follow the main wagon-road up to the Broken Back spread Charley led us around these back trails through the hills so that Quiros would think we had been hard at work out on the range. By nightfall we reached the corral where they did their brand doctoring and set off again the next morning.

Most of my life had been spent in the saddle, so I'm a naturally proficient rider, but I couldn't get up much speed on my broken-down mustang. I was worried he might give up the ghost altogether, so had to nurse him along. I'm a man of average height, about five eight, and lightly built, so, of course, that helps if a horse doesn't have to carry too much weight. But he was blowing hard as we struggled to keep up with the others in our wild bunch.

'Hell take it!' Charley Bowdler cried, as he reached a rise and whirled his mount around.

At first I thought his horse might have trod on a rattler, but as I rode up to join the others I saw what the commotion was. Down in a dip were a dozen Mescalero Apaches, the sun flashing on their knives as they hacked away the hindquarters of a steer.

'Look at that,' Shoot yelled, 'helping 'emselves to our beef afore our very eyes.'

'We gotta teach 'em a lesson,' young

37

Windy agreed, drawing his revolver from his belt, standing in his stirrups and brandishing it. 'Come on, boys.'

Before we could advise caution he set off pell-mell down the rise, closely followed by Shoot. They were hollering like a couple of savages, themselves.

'Dang fools!' Charley hung on to his bronc as he pulled his carbine from the saddle boot, and taciturn and sullen Dan, by his side, did the same. 'Why don't they wait for the word?'

The only thing to do was charge after them, so I grabbed hold of my Winchester, levering the first of its twelve slugs out of the magazine and into the breech, raked my mustang's sides and went after them at the gallop.

By now the Mescaleros had jumped to their feet in readiness, raising rifles and fitting arrows swiftly into small bows. Windy pirouetted from his horse and thrashed groaning on the ground hanging on to a lance stuck through his abdomen.

Shoot fired his revolver point blank into the brave who had thrown it, but another of the warriors leaped up behind him and wrestled him to the ground. Charley and Dan charged into the raiding party firing as

38

accurately as the motion of the galloping broncs would allow. I pulled my Winchester tight into my shoulder and managed to wing a young warrior with my first bullet, making him stumble.

But the next thing I knew my mustang shrieked with pain and terror as a slug from the Indian's ancient rifle tore into his chest. He cartwheeled, throwing me from the saddle to hit the ground with a thud, knocking my breath from my body. For moments I was winded, the air gurgling out of me, and all I could do was watch my poor bronc on his back, spouting blood as he kicked his last.

All around me was a mêlée of fighting, thudding, grunting, grimacing men, some in feathers, some in Stetsons, and, as I lay there, it all looked like some slow-moving frieze – Charley, on horseback, laying about him with his rifle, the others shooting, stabbing, or leaping at each other to grapple for supremacy.

Suddenly, as my breath came back, I saw a lithe, half-naked Mescalero standing over me, his arm raised as he swung a vicious-looking tomahawk blade at my skull. I managed to twist my head aside and the weapon-head sank into the soft ground. I caught hold of his wrists as he knelt over me and raised the tomahawk to try again. For ten seconds we were locked together in a battle for life or death.

The Mescalero grunted a few words which I knew enough of their lingo to know meant, 'White Eyes, you will soon be dead.'

As if to prove this he broke my hold, raised the skull-cracker and slashed again at my face. Again I jerked my head aside and the blade cut through my silk neckerchief and jammed into the earth.

'You ain't gonna kill *me* like a pig,' I grunted back.

I got my knee up under him and with a huge effort I tossed him over my head. I had lost my carbine and I didn't have time to draw my revolvers because he dragged me tumbling with him. I grabbed at the nearest thing I saw, a fallen scalping-knife.

Once more we locked in a battle of strength, but this time I was on top, holding him down as his dark eyes in a face the colour of burnished walnut stared into mine with defiant menace. He had my knife-hand in his grip and I was hanging on for grim life to his tomahawk. I might not be so lucky at his third try. My only weapon available was my teeth so I bit them into his nose. When he howled with surprise and pain, he loosened his grip on my wrist: so I jerked the knife back and plunged it deep into his chest with all my might.

The blade must have pierced his heart for he choked on his blood as I lay gasping upon him and watched him die, the light leave his eyes.

But there was no time to hang around. I scrambled to my feet, easing both of my Lightning .38s from my hips, and, as a screaming Mescalero leaped from the top of a rock upon me, I fired both six-guns simultaneously. He did his death dance in mid-air.

I spun around, but the Indians had had enough and those still on their feet were backing away, leaping on to their ponies and, shouting cries of defiance, racing away. We emptied our cylinders in a final volley. As they galloped away across a crest another of them bit the dust.

'Whoo!' Charley gave a drawn-out whistle as he sucked on air and looked about us. Windy, with the lance struck through him, was sprawled dead, his face a rictus of pain. And five of the Mescaleros appeared to be fatalities, too. 'We sho showed them a thang or two.'

He stood with his carbine still gripped by the barrel, the butt blood-streaked where he had used it as a club. Dan was on one knee clutching at a knife-wound in his upper arm. Charley went to help him up. 'You OK, pal?'

'I hope so,' Dan grunted. 'If these young fools hadn't charged at 'em we coulda picked 'em off from the ridge.'

Shoot looked sheepish. 'That was Windy's fault. I had ta go after him.'

'Waal,' Charley drawled, 'Windy sure learned from his mistake. He ain't gonna make no more of 'em.'

Behind him one of the Apaches stirred, his face a mask as he slowly raised his knife, aimed for one last throw at Charley's back. I fired past Bowdler's waist and put a slug between the warrior's eyes.

'He wanted to take you with him to the Happy Hunting Ground,' I said, as he fell back.

We went to take a look at the other dead, to make sure they were. Two of them were as stunted as pygmies, their sun-blackened bodies emaciated, thick hair hanging about grim, almost primeval, faces. One was wearing a cavalry captain's ceremonial helmet, with its crest of horsehair.

'I wonder who he took that from
poor devil from Fort Stanton.'

'Yep,' Shoot said, and pointed to s⌐
a belt. 'These boys had been raiding. Dam⌐
Injins! They never learn.'

'Still, they've left behind a few horses.'
Charley uncoiled his rawhide lariat and
rode away to lasso one of the dead Indians'
mounts. He brought him back and called,
'This pinto'll make a good replacement for
you, Angel.'

'Thanks.' I dragged my saddle from the
dead horse. He was better off out of it, his
sufferings over. I slung it over the sturdy
pinto. 'What we gonna do about all these
dead?'

'We'll take Windy back to bury him.
Normally I'd leave these others for the
coyotes, but, no,' Charley mused. 'I think
we'll sling all these stiffies over their ponies
and take 'em back to the ranch. It'll show
Quiros we ain't been wasting our time.
We've been earnin' our pay, yes, sir.'

'We might as well take those steaks they
were carving, too,' Shoot piped up. 'They'll
make a change to that slop George
Washington dishes up.'

George, a black freed-slave, had been
brought to New Mexico by Quiros, his

43

rmer owner, and worked as ranch cook and yard hand. He certainly didn't excel at the culinary arts, that was for sure.

It was dusk by the time we trailed back. A warning bell started clanging as we were sighted and Quiros came out on to his veranda, a formidable and bulky sight, draped in a travelling cloak and slouch hat. Beside him stood the shotgun-toting Harry. Behind them I glimpsed Belle, watching from the lighted doorway.

'Where the hell you been all week?' Quiros bellowed, puffing on his cigar. He looked like an angry snorting bull.

'Where you think?' Charley yelled back. 'Out on the range.'

'You damnable liar. I know where you've been, down in White Oaks, painting the town red.'

We pulled our procession of horses to a halt in the dusty half-lit yard.

'Oh, yeah? So what the fugg you think these are? We've been defending your stock from raiding 'pache, risking our lives, you mealy-mouthed bastard. Windy's dead, Dan's wounded, and here's some of the savages we kilt.'

Quiros stepped down and swaggered across the yard to take a look at the bodies

44

slung over the broncs. 'Well,' he muttered, 'my apologies. It looks like you might be telling the truth.'

'Yeah,' Charley sneered, 'it looks like we might, don't it? We took on a raiding party who'd brought down one of your steers. How many you say there were, Shoot? A good twenty of 'em 'ginst four of us. Hand to hand fightin'. It's lucky any of us survived. But we made 'em run. And for what, the few shekels you pay us? An' to come back to your lousy accusations.'

For the first time since I'd met him Monsieur Quiros looked flustered. 'It's just that somebody said they'd seen you down at White Oaks and a man had been killed. Sorry, boys, you done well. Tonight I'll have George break open a cask of whiskey.'

I glanced up behind his back at Belle and flashed her a smile. She took my breath away. A real stunner as the hurricane lamp in the room behind her back lit her blonde hair like a halo, and silhouetted the curves of her body through the flimsy white dress. She gave me a scoffing grin, just the tips of her front teeth gleaming in those loose and decadently painted lips. She tossed her head, slowly turned and went inside, the screen door banging after her.

45

'Jeez!' I gave a low whistle through my lips. 'What an apparition! What a gal to come home to.'

Five

We tossed George Washington the fly-buzzing gunny sack of steaks and ribs and told
him to get them sizzling. He couldn't make
much of a mistake apart from burning them
to a cinder. The jug of corn whiskey was
rough and gut-twisting, but it set my fingers
racing across the guitar strings. We had a
raucously merry evening, celebrating the
fact of still being alive and our scalps intact.
The Mex miners joined the party in full
throat as I gave them the tricky *'Celito
Lindo'* and the rousing *'El Caballero'*. Their
voices and my playing must have drifted
from the bunkhouse across the yard to
where the Quiroses sat on their porch,
especially when we went into the
melancholy and traditional song of farewell,
'La Paloma'. I guess they felt somewhat left
out of things.

The next morning I had a brain- and
body-numbing hangover like I'd been
trampled by a herd of steers. That corn
whiskey can sure getcha! But it was Sunday

so we could lie on our bunks and relax all day. I had the Mex washerwomen scrub my shirt and jeans, which quickly dried in the summer sun, and I peered into a little cracked glass and used my cut-throat razor to shave away six days of stubble. Although I was a *genizaro*, a mixed-blood, I was lucky in that I had inherited my mother's good looks and ice-blue eyes, although my hair was as black and thick as my daddy's once had been. I say lucky in that, as anybody knows, to have the dark-blooded looks of a Mexican-Indian makes a man a second-class citizen in this country. Lucky too, that, let's face it, my good looks meant that I had never had much trouble finding girlfriends. If I sat on the steps outside a saloon and plucked a few airs on my guitar I soon had a little group around me, the *señoritas* making shy doe-eyes from behind their fluttering fans. They were ripe for the plucking by a handsome *caballero*. So, I generally plucked them and rode on my way, hoping I hadn't left any little ones to be remembered by. None of these *queridas* had instilled me with the hankering to settle down with them in a *casa* in some dusty New Mexican town. But Belle was different. She had hit me like the shock of the new and it is true to say I was fixated, or fascinated, by her. But how, I wondered, as I looked into my somewhat bloodshot eyes in the little mirror that day, was I to get close to her?

The answer came with an invitation from the ranch- and mine-owner delivered by the shotgun-toting Harry.

'The boss wants ya to go over tonight and play for them.'

'Oh, yeah,' I sneered. 'Is he planning to pay me?' But there was only one payment I needed, a certain plum who needed picking. My heart began to beat as fast as my guitar strings at the prospect.

'Have a drink, Angel.' Mr Quiros was in an expansive mood as he stood on his porch and opened a bottle. 'Good of you to come. Belle was intrigued by the music last night. We both were. Hope you might play for us some.'

'Ain't in a drinkin' or playin' mood,' I said, grumpily. 'That potato lightning really hit me.'

'Aw, this is only wine. The best. Just what you need.'

He passed me a glass of sparkling French Chardonnay. 'Best of luck to you.'

Yeah, I'm gonna need it, I thought,

49

wondering where Belle had gotten to.

'Music is something we greatly miss, both of us, since being stuck out here in these backwoods. Company grows burdensome if it isn't spiced with good conversation. But who can one converse with intelligently in these parts?'

'Beats me,' I agreed, coughing as I got the bubbles of the wine up my nose. 'A hoss is generally better company than most of the *hombres* around here.'

'Yes, I sense you are a man of some discernment.'

'I surely am,' I said, thinking once again of his wife. 'I been badly undersold so far in life. Ain't achieved the potential that oughta be mine.'

'And I, I'm an exile from my motherland, la belle France. All I have are these wines to remind me.' He rambled on, licking his fleshy red lips, chopping them with ecstasy as he recalled the wines of Burgundy, the Loire and chateau-bottled Rhônes. 'This is the best I can offer you.'

'Tastes fine to me.' Indeed, I was glad to see him already opening another bottle because it packed quite a heady kick, that Chardonnay. 'Not having tried much of this stuff cain't really compare...'

'Oh, you don't know what you are missing, Angel. And another thing I miss is culture, books, art galleries, museums. If only I could see again those Titians, Berninis, Michelangelos, Domenicos ... you know, my soul is like a plant that withers for lack of nourishment.'

The guy looked plenty well-nourished to me. 'So, if you don't like it here, why don't you go back to your own country?'

'That is what we plan to do once I have accumulated enough capital. But, why do I bother talking to you? I doubt if you comprehend what I say? Always it is like throwing pearls before swine.'

I noted, rather ruefully, the 'we'. And I wasn't too keen on being included as one of the swine. 'Well, good luck to *you*, Alexandre,' I said, familiarly, taking another bite of the bottle. I twirled my guitar on my knee and started strumming a few chords in the hope it might entice the lady on to the veranda. I didn't relish listening to this fat creep all night.

I was concentrating on my fingering and when I looked up she was standing there, the shadows playing on her pale face and hair, an ankle-length gown of white lace over satin clinging to her body. *'Madre*

Dios!' I exclaimed, startled by the sight of her. 'I didn't hear you come out.'

'She is rather feline, isn't she?' Quiros beamed, touching dainty fingers to his greasy curled hair. 'She moves as quietly as a cat.'

'Go on playing, Angel' she whispered in a husky voice, and sat on a nearby chair. 'It's nice.'

'*You're My Angel*' seemed a suitable love-lament to serenade her with, but whether she understood the Spanish words I was not sure. She certainly must have caught the longing in my voice and eyes.

'You've got a good singing voice, Angel,' she remarked when I ceased, to quench my thirst with another glass. 'But, don't you know any American songs?'

'No, they ain't my style.' I smiled at her, raising the glass. 'I'm a hot-blooded Latin.'

'Really?' She made a motion of her eyebrows and a flicker of a smile. 'So, sing some more.'

It was no hardship, something I could do with ease, run my fingers across the strings, out there in the cool air, under the stars, tell her, in my own language, that I wanted her. And she lapped it up as I stared at her. I was trying to discern in the lamplight whether

her eyes were green or amber, or a mixture of the two, like those of a lynx, or mountain cat, glowing in the dark as she prowled.

The massive bulk of Quiros was suddenly raised by its owner and I thought, for alarmed moments, that he'd had enough of this blatant flirtation with his wife. He staggered, scraping his rocker back.

'It's getting cold out here. Let's go inside.' I watched him lurch towards the screen door and got the impression he had been drinking before my arrival and was already half-drunk. 'I've got a *carafon* of good earthy Mexican red,' he bellowed, leading the way. 'It will complement the white beautifully.'

It was true that in the mountains at that altitude the heat of the day is quickly dispelled by darkness, and a chill downdraught from the jagged mountain wall across the trail had hit us. Belle and I stood to follow him, as we did so I slapped my cupped hand hard on to her hip. She jumped like a startled mare and glared at me angrily. But her face softened and she smiled at me, reaching down to clasp my offending hand in hers.

'Just take it easy, cowboy,' she murmured, and opened the screen door for herself. 'Don't get excited. You're only here to

53

entertain us. Remember that.'

I guess Belle thought she had a duty to her husband to try to deter my ardour, but, in that case, what was that hand-squeeze for? Or, was she really a teaser? When we got in Quiros was already glugging down a tumbler of dark red wine from the *carafon*. I took a sip of the glass he offered me, but it tasted foul. Maybe I'd let *him* do the drinking.

The inside of the house was nothing special; a table and chairs, a battered horsehair sofa, a few pictures and books, not that I was interested in that. Through a door I could see a kitchen.

'You cook for yourselves?' I asked. 'You don't trust George Washington's efforts?'

'Yes, I prefer French cuisine. Subtle spices and herbs,' Quiros said and rattled on about various recipes he favoured.

Belle went into the kitchen and returned with some refreshments, goat's cheese, chunks of cold spiced toast, sliced tomatoes bathed in olive oil. 'Help yourself.'

I sat at the table opposite Quiros while Belle sprawled on the sofa and pulled the skirt of her dress around her knees. I could see she was wearing white stockings. All she needed was a headdress and veil and she'd look like some durned bride.

We chatted about the attack by the Mescaleros and I described my role, exaggerating it somewhat, and also, like Charley, the size of the horde of savages we had fought off. 'Kit Carson punished the tribe in the War,' I said. 'He put them and the Navajo to the fire and sword. Nobody thought they would ask for more. They got that damn great reservation in the mountains stretching for countless miles. But I guess a new generation of young braves has grown up and they want vengeance.'

'They'll learn the hard way. They'll regret it.' The voice of Quiros had a distinct drunken slur. 'Tomorrow I'll ride to Fort Stanton and demand action. They gotta be punished again.'

'It's the first time I've killed a man up close' – I conveniently forgot about Blackbeard at White Oaks as I described how I had slid the razor-sharp knife into the Indian's ribs – 'I never thought it could be so easy.'

'Did you enjoy doing it?' Belle was licking at her painted lips like she was some predator thirsting for blood. 'Surely it must have excited you?'

'Hell, no, what do you think I am?' I

protested, and then I grinned at her. 'Well, I suppose, at the time, it excites you to win.'

Our eyes seemed to clash sparks off each other as we spoke. When she suggested some English songs and began humming the refrains, I tried plucking the tune on the guitar, and we laughed as we tried to capture the elusive melody. Quiros joined in, bellowing some French number in his deep voice, roaring, like us, with merriment. It seemed like we three had a natural empathy.

But, as the evening wore on, and I asked them whether they wanted children, he began to get bitter and bellicose.

'If I had a daughter,' he claimed, 'I would advise her to become a whore. I would defy her to find a worthier profession. What better than to live in the lap of luxury and drunken debauchery?'

He giggled at his wit. I glanced at Belle and she raised her eyebrows as if to suggest that in his cups her husband often came out with similarly ridiculous statements. Suddenly, I could hardly believe my eyes when I saw that her right hand was massaging above her dress her formidable bosom, and, as I stared in disbelief, she snaked her fingers down between her thighs to stroke at herself with such sensuousness that her eyes became cloudy with desire.

I looked, apprehensively, at Quiros, who was rocking back on the heels of his chair, puffing at his cigar, his own eyes heavy-lidded and half-closed. I realized that from his position he could not see what Belle was doing, his view cut off by the back of the sofa.

'Has the silly bitch gone to sleep?' he drawled.

'No,' I replied, my mouth dry, as I watched her raise the hem of her dress so that her milk-white thighs above the stocking-tops were revealed, and her fingers began acting even more lubriciously. 'No, I don't think so.'

Her eyes were locked, mockingly with mine, as Quiros burped and began, 'The trouble with Belle is...' Suddenly the chair legs slipped, glasses crashed as he tried to recover himself, but he tumbled down backwards with an almighty slam, hitting his head against the brickwork of the fireplace.

'Jesus!' I cried out, jumping to one knee to take a look at him. 'Christ, I thought for a minute he was dead. No, he's breathing.' I slapped his face, trying to bring him round, the jowls slapping like a baggy pig's bladder against my hand, but it was no good. 'He's out cold. He's got a nasty crack on the back of the head. It's bleeding. We better try to move him.'

'Leave him,' his wife snarled, without moving from the sofa. 'He's drunk. Not unusual.'

'Still, perhaps–'

'Move him? You're joking. He weighs a ton.' Her voice took on a softer tone as she murmured, 'Relax, Angel.'

I froze for moments, staring at the recumbent Quiros. Then I rose and looked down at her. She had her dress up high now and both her hands were inside her pantalettes as she stared at me, wantonly, crazily, begging me. I didn't need any more urging. An electric shock seared up my spine. I went round to her. I grabbed at her hips, tore the pantalettes off, then ripped apart that crazy mockery of a wedding dress, and, as her breasts tumbled free, I bit my teeth into the nipples, sucking at them like a man demented. 'Careful,' she gasped. But I was not in a mood to be careful. Belle groaned as I slammed myself into her and Quiros, lying a few feet away, was forgotten.

Six

The solid double-barrels of a shotgun jammed into my back as I left the ranch house.

'Been having fun?' a voice growled.

'Sure. A pleasant evening.'

'I bet it was.'

'What you want, Harry? It's late.'

'I seen what you and her were doing. I been watching. She oughta draw the curtain.'

'You' – I turned, pushing the shotgun aside, raising my right fist – 'you dirty snooper.'

'Yeah,' he chuckled. 'I like to keep an eye on what's going on.'

His face was shaded by the hatbrim, but beneath the heavy moustache I could see a glimmer of fang-like teeth in the moonlight. I lowered my fist. 'Why don't you crawl back under your stone?'

'Where's Quiros? Asleep?'

'You could say that. He fell off his chair, KO'd himself on the hearth.'

'Yeah?' Harry, a stocky, middle-aged man, in his black outfit and shirt, lowered the twelve-gauge. 'I better take a look.'

'All right,' I sighed. The light in the living-room had been doused, but a candle was flickering in the kitchen. Harry hammered on the side door.

'Mrs Quiros, are you OK?'

There was no reply so he shoved inside. Belle was sitting at the kitchen table, her legs protruding from a loose housecoat. She was daubing some kind of cream on her face.

'What do you want?'

'Angel here says your husband's had an accident. I better take a look at him.'

'Help yourself.' She poured herself a glass of wine as her eyes met mine. 'He's still breathing.'

'Boss. Wake up.' In the living-room Harry knelt beside the corpulent Frenchman and started slapping his face. He put a hand behind his head and looked at blood on his palm. 'I don't like the look of that cut. You better get some water and bandages.'

Expressionless, Belle pointed to a kitchen cupboard and I found what I needed. Harry bathed the cut through the greasy curls and tied a bandage tight.

'What hit me?' Quiros groaned as his eyes fluttered open. 'What you doin' in my house?'

'You had a fall,' Harry said. 'Come on, we're gonna help you up, get you to bed.'

We hauled the vast whale of a man into an adjoining room and threw him on to a brass bedstead. 'Thanks, boys,' he murmured as he closed his eyes again.

Belle was standing in the doorway watching, the candle-holder in her hand. As we turned to go she gave a down-turned twitch of her lips. 'He don't leave me much room, does he?'

'Good night, Mrs Quiros.' I brushed past her, flicking her a wink. 'Sleep tight.'

When we stepped outside Harry caught hold of my arm. 'If Quiros finds out what's goin' on, he'll kill you.'

'How's he gonna do that, Harry?' I asked, softly. 'You gonna squeal?'

'I might. Or I might not. Just don't upset me. Stay outa my way. I'm the right-hand man here. Don't think you can muscle in.'

'I ain't interested in your job, Harry. Once I git my month's wages I'm outa here headed for Santa Fe.' I slung my guitar over my shoulder and ambled over to the bunk-house. 'You've no need to worry about me.

And there's no use you trying to blackmail me about tonight, because I don't have nuthin' worth having.'

'Maybe,' he growled. 'Not yet you don't.'

As he strode away to his separate shack I wondered what he meant by that 'maybe'.

To reach Fort Stanton we had to follow for fifty miles a rough trail that forded two rivers. I had been detailed to drive the two-horse buggy. Belle, in a tight-fitting dress of pink candy stripe, carrying a parasol, sat up on the box between me and her large husband on the far side. Harry and Charley rode along beside us. Shoot and Dan had been left to guard the mine. It took us two days. We stopped off and stayed the night at Milner's sawmill.

'Hot dang!' Charley yelled, sardonically, as the blockhouse and stockade of Fort Stanton finally hove into view. 'Ain't we lucky we got Uncle Sam's boys to protect us.'

'Yeah,' Shotgun Harry, another ex-Reb, growled. 'Never thought we'd be askin' some damn Yankees fer help.'

'Boys.' Quiros lit another of his big cigars. 'The war's been over a long time. I pay my taxes and it's the job of these bluebellies to keep the Mescaleros on their reservation.'

In her freshly laundered dress, lace at its cuffs and throat, a little bowler hat pinned to the top of her shiny gold hair, her lace-gloved fingers pertly holding the parasol, Belle acted as cool as a cucumber. Occasionally, when the wagon swayed, I felt the warmth of her thigh against mine. But generally she acted aloof and debonair towards me as if two nights before had never occurred.

The wooden gates of pointed logs were drawn open for us and we drove through and across the parade ground past a body of parading infantry. I noticed the horny leers of the soldiers, the grins and nudges as they stared at her. 'Hey!' One gave a low whistle 'What a beaut!' The others, with their shouldered muskets, cackled, as the sergeant called them to order. Belle stared straight ahead, unconcerned.

Harry helped the portly Quiros, attired in a baggy linen suit and Panama hat, to climb down, and the Frenchman offered his own hand to his wife. She hung on to his arm as he led her towards the office of Colonel Dudley. The colonel was wearing a helmet with a horsehair plume like the one we had found on the Messy warrior, and in his blue frockcoat, sash, sabre and ribbons of rank, he looked more like somebody out of a comic opera than the leader of fighting troops. He was pompous with it, too.

'Well?' He hummed and hawed as we were served sherry. 'I'm not sure I have the men to spare to mount an expedition into the mountains. Right now I'm trying to keep the lid on the feuding going on down at Lincoln.'

'White men and white women' – Quiros put his arm around Belle's waist and gave her a squeeze – 'are under threat to their lives. We demand protection. Good God, man, all you have to do is give the Mescaleros a pasting. They'll soon learn to keep out of our hair.'

'I'm afraid I'll need authority to mount a military campaign like that. We are trying to solve the Indian problem not exacerbate it. However, if your men put in their reports I will forward them to the governor with my recommendations.'

'Meanwhile,' Quiros fumed, 'the Apaches are free to run off my cattle and kill us with impunity. What kind of problem solving do you call that?'

'I can only do the best with the troops under my command,' Dudley blustered.

'Useless cowardly piece of horse shit,'

Quiros muttered, as we left his office. 'We're wasting our time here.'

The next day I drove the rig back across the River Bonito for twenty miles or so to White Oaks which we reached late evening. Belle wanted to stock up on supplies and buy herself some new dresses and Quiros needed some crates of wine, cigars, mining equipment, and ammunition.

White Oaks' narrow main street was packed with wagons, horses, mule-trains, miners in dusty denims going hither and thither, or climbing up to their shafts that pocked the steep valley walls like so many holes in a Swiss cheese.

Belle suddenly squeezed my knee with her gloved fingers as her husband clambered down – and her touch shot through me like a bolt of lightning.

'Angel can carry my shopping,' she called. 'Where shall we meet you, Alexandre?'

'At the Claremont. I'll book rooms overnight.'

Belle led me through the bustle to McGinty's Merchandise Emporium where she busied herself buying coffee-beans, spices, jars of pickles and dried apples, while I loaded the wagon with sacks of flour and grain. She paid cash from a little silver embroidered reticule that hung from her wrist.

We were off again. This time she went tripping along the wooden sidewalk in her high-buttoned bootees, her hips swaying, as shoddily-dressed miners, bull-whackers and drunks lurching from the saloons gawped at her with awe and stood back to make way as she rustled past them in her bell-shaped summer dress.

A shop bell dinged and we stepped inside a ladies' haberdasher's and fashion house, where dummies displayed the latest fashions and the counter was loaded with rolls of materials and ribbons.

The satin evening-dresses and ridiculous feathered hats were much in demand by the 'prairie nymphs' who flocked to the town in the wake of the free-spending miners. I watched with interest as a bevy of these exotic birds cooed and squealed over a display of the latest Parisian basques and stockings. Meanwhile, Belle was being measured for a new dress in green velvet.

'Put these on the buggy, will you?' she commanded me, haughtily, pointing to a pile of boxes and parcels.

I gave a snort, but did as she bid, and waited outside. Who, I wondered, did she think I was, some skivvy?

'Where now?' I asked, when she came outside.

'I've bought you a new bandanna.' She handed me the silk scarf empatterned in pink and purple. 'That one of yours is badly torn.'

'Yeah, that's where that 'pache nearly put his tomahawk through my throat.'

'Really, you do live dangerously!' Belle gave a supercilious toss of her blonde hair as she surveyed me. 'One does get a little tired of *Parfum de Vaquero*. You could do with a new shirt and underwear.'

'Gee, thanks, ma'am,' I crowed, sarcastically.

'When was the last time you had a bath?'

'Let me see now.' I frowned. 'That musta been last year. No, maybe the year before.' In fact, it had only been a month ago and I'd splashed myself in the tank since then.

'Come along. I'll get you fitted out and show you the bath house.'

Now, I would be the first to agree that most *vaqueros* stink worse than their horses, but I didn't quite understand why she was putting on these lah-di-dah airs and keeping her distance from me.

'Sure, that'll be fine and dandy, ma'am,' I

agreed as I strode beside her, glancing around to make sure there was nobody in the bustling crowd who was watching us. By now it was nearly dark. I hauled her by one arm into an alleyway, slamming her up against a wall of shiplap boards.

Belle gave a screech as she tried to fight me off. 'What do you think you're doing?'

'What the hell you *think* I'm doing?' I had her pinned there as I snatched up her candy-striped dress and underskirts. 'Ain't this what you're wanting?' I thrust my mouth on to her lips.

'No! Get off me!' She turned her face away to avoid my hungry kisses. 'Don't! Everybody can see.'

I glanced along at the entry to the street, at the people passing but nobody seemed to notice us in the dusk. 'Too bad,' I grunted. 'We better get on with it, hadn't we?'

'You brute! How dare you?' But her protestations became more feeble. 'Oh, my God,' she groaned, as she hung on to my neck. 'This is terrible.'

'You started it,' I gasped.

'You!' she cried, a short while later, straightening her dress. 'You're an animal. This is all you want me for.'

'And you don't? Come on, Belle, we better

get outa here.' I strode to the alley entrance, looked about me and jerked my head for her to follow. 'That's funny. Damn me, we been up against the wall of the Claremont Hotel.'

When she joined me I grinned at her and said, 'I think I'll miss out on the bath-house today. You better get used to *Parfum de Vaquero.*'

Alexandre Quiros was sat at a side table alongside the wall. He had loosened his floppy bow-tie beneath his flabby chins to give him more chance to breathe, and was mopping at his brow with a kerchief. It occurred to me that he must have been sitting about two feet away from us on the other side of that thin board wall. Could he have overheard our words?

'Ah, Belle.' He beckoned us with his cigar to join him. 'Have you done all you wanted to do?'

'Yes, I think so,' she replied, looking hot and flustered as she adjusted the little hat on her head and removed her lace gloves. 'I'm dying for a drink.'

'I've just what the doctor ordered, darling.' He waggled a finger at the barkeep. 'Had it put in a bucket of ice.'

The 'keep came over with a bottle of French champagne and poured us all a glass. Quiros handed him a greenback and ordered, 'Keep 'em coming. We've got a thirst.'

'What's the celebration?' I raised my glass to him and Belle.

'Celebration? There's no celebration. This is how I and my wife are accustomed to live. We have expensive tastes.'

'You don't say,' I said. 'So, bottoms up.'

Quiros certainly liked to flaunt his wealth, but when a dark-eyed Mexican peasant woman in a ragged shawl, a baby in her arm, three toddlers wound around her legs, came around the tables begging, he fluttered his fingers at her and told her to clear off.

'*Señor*, I have thirteen children,' she pleaded, pointing fingers to her mouth. 'They are hungry.'

'Isn't that your own fault? Why do you have so many children?'

'*Señor*, I love my husband, that is why.'

'Well, I love my cigar, but I take it out now and then.' Quiros's breasts and bellies shook with laughter and he flipped the *paisane* a few cents to get rid of her. 'These people,' he sighed.

'She sure didn't get your joke.'

Quiros saw a businessman of his acquaint-

70

ance at the bar, and, failing to catch his eye, waddled through the throng of gamblers and drinkers to go talk to him.

'So,' I asked Belle. 'How you enjoyin' your trip so far?'

'You dirty bastard. This must never happen again.' She wetted her handkerchief and rubbed furtively at a damp stain. 'Look what you done to my dress. I'm sure he noticed. Angel, this has got to stop.'

I didn't have time to reason with her because at that moment there was the loud clap of a gunshot up close. A slug whistled past my head and smashed through the shiplap wall!

As the cloud of gunsmoke cleared I saw a stocky little miner standing at the bar, his carbine aimed at me and smoking. It was the friend of the big Blackbeard I had killed not many days before. 'I warned you to stay out of White Oaks and especially this saloon, Alvorado. Oh, yes, I know who you are. We don't need no cheap murderin' card-sharps in here.'

As the shot clapped out I had instinctively ducked and pushed Belle aside. Her chair had tumbled over and she was half-upturned on the floor, waving her stockinged legs, trying to right herself. 'Stay down,' I hissed at her, as I rose to face the man, or men, at the bar, for there seemed to be two or three of them, and others, while getting back out of the line of fire were standing staring at me like a band of snarling wolves.

'Let me handle this.' A tall, gangling man, with a long, bearded face and an eyepatch, was standing beside the miner. 'George was my friend.' He was wearing a long duster coat and drew it aside to reveal a big Remington .44 stuffed into his thick leather belt. 'Come on, you yeller, killin', card-cheat. Let's see how fast you are.'

Three glasses of champagne had given me a sense of false bravado. 'There don't seem no point in arguing with you numbheads,' I said, and went for my .38s. The beauty of a double action is you save fractions of a second by not having to cock it, or them, and I kept them and my holsters well oiled. It undoubtedly saved my life. I was that fraction faster than the two at the bar. My Lightnings were out and firing from the hips – the eight explosions barrelled together in one long noise – as I sent four bullets from each revolver hitting their separate targets.

The tall man in the duster coat and the little miner stood there transfixed, their faces agonized, without even getting a shot in. Their weapons fell from their useless hands as they, too, dropped, rolling to the floor and spurting blood.

I peered around me through the black powder-smoke, but any who might have been thinking of taking me, hands hovering over guns in their belts, seemed to be changing their minds.

'Look out!' Belle screamed, and I immediately knelt for cover as a shot rang out and smashed the bottle of champagne on the table.

I looked up at the balcony and saw a gunman with a carbine standing there as another shot cracked out. He gave a spasm, and toppled forward over the banister to crash down on to a card table. Out cold. A hole in his gut. It was then I saw Quiros standing by the bar, his pistol pointed upwards and smoking.

'He was putting my wife in mortal danger,' he bellowed to the hushed crowd. 'What's more he ruined a damned expensive bottle of wine.'

Belle had been showered with glass and champagne. When I helped her up she pulled away, angrily brushing herself down. 'Gracious heavens! I'm beginning to think it's not a good idea being around you.'

'*Sacré bleu!*' Quiros ambled over blowing down the long barrel of his ancient powder-and-ball duelling pistol with its curious birdclaw grip. 'That was some shooting, *mon ami.*'

'Yours, too. That fella would have had me if you hadn't spotted him.'

Harry and Charley came pushing in through the saloon's batwing doors, wanting to know what had happened.

'Don't worry,' Quiros laughed. 'We took care of things. Where were you boys when you were needed?'

Harry stood with his shotgun in his hands scowling surlily through his moustache. 'We jest went across to git some baccy.'

'That's another two notches on your gun, Angel,' Charley yelled, going over to my eye-patched assailant and taking his Remington. 'You're starting to make quite a name for yourself.'

'He called you a cheat.'

'Yeah, he did.' I met Belle's accusing eyes. 'That's why I shot him.' I shrugged my shoulders at Quiros. 'You know these drunken miners, they don't like losing.'

'They don't like cheats.'

'Calm down, *ma petite*,' Quiros soothed

74

and seated her. 'Let's open a couple more bottles.'

The town sheriff, a burly man named Beaver Smith, bustled in to find out what was going on. Most men in the packed saloon agreed that I had been fired on and it had been a fair fight. We had been too fast for them.

'It's no big deal, Sheriff,' Quiros said. 'You get gunfights every night, don't you?'

'That man's a troublemaker,' Smith jabbed a stubby finger at me. 'I've a mind to lock him up. As for the rest of you, I'd advise you to get outa town, pronto. This is a mining town an' they're prone to act by miners' law – he wouldn't be the first *hombre* to be found hanging high. Him being Mex, too.'

'I ain't Mexican. I'm a Texican. My mother was a solid white protestant Texas girl. Her family was from Bavaria or someplace, over in Europe. Don't go calling me Mex.'

'A 'breed? That's worse.' Beaver Smith cleared his throat and aimed a gob of chawin' baccy at a spitoon. 'You frontier 'breeds are all card-sharps, thieves and murderers. I wouldn't trust you further than I could spit, pal.'

'Come on, Sheriff. No need for harsh words. Have a drink.' Quiros poured him a wine and pressed a folded greenback into his paw. 'Angel and these other men work for me and nobody's running us out of town.'

'I'm thinkin' of your own safety, suh.' Beaver smacked his lips as he downed the drink and pocketed the bribe. 'Ah, well, don't say I didn't warn you.'

He went over to examine the dead, confiscate their personal property, before they were dragged out by their bootheels and a saloon lackey began mopping up the blood.

The professor of piano had begun tickling the ivories again and it was time for the evening show, a troupe of girls prancing on to the stage, kicking their legs, screeching and somersaulting, showing their frills and furbelows to the randy miners.

Charley examined the Remington .44. 'Hey, I think I'll hang on to this.'

Belle watched coolly, ignoring me. The gunfight had jangled my nerves and I was ill at ease, like a cat on a hot tin roof expecting an attack from every quarter. I kept my back to the wall and my twin Lightnings loose in their holsters. They were the new short-barrelled revolvers, which, in my opinion, gave a man extra seconds of advantage in whisking 'em out. They were nickel-plated with studded gutta percha butts which lent a better grip and prevented the termites from eating 'em. I made sure they were fully loaded from the lower ammo belt around my waist. In the higher belt I kept my brass .44's for my Winchester.

We were served steaks and sweet potatoes, primed with red hot chilli peppers. I played some monte but wasn't in the mood to concentrate and lost my last few dollars. I didn't even have enough to buy myself a beer. The old green-eyed goddess was working her evil tricks on me as I sat and watched Alexandre Quiros swagger over to the roulette table and take a stance. Belle stood by his side urging him on. He seemed to be on a winning streak and I could see her teeth and eyes flashing in the light of the whale-oil lamps as he raked in his chips. The big shot with the big cigar. His classy dame.

I took a stroll around the town, noting the shifty looks men kept throwing me. I didn't need this kind of notoriety. Quiros had booked us rooms above the saloon, he and Belle in a centre one, Charley and Harry in one on the right-hand side, me on the other side, for protection.

I turned in early, about midnight, and hung my revolvers from the bedpost, but I couldn't get any sleep, what with the noise of whores clip-clopping back and forth, doors banging, screams of arguments over cash, and the clamour downstairs.

It must have been about two a.m. when I heard Quiros and Belle enter their room. Through the thin wall I could hear their conversation. It sounded like he had had quite a night. Their light went out and then there were mutterings and rustlings and Belle gave a giggle as the bedsprings groaned under their weight. The springs began to creak rhythmically, and there was a lot of gasping and Belle started to moan.

I tried to cut them out, jamming the pillow down over my ears. But listening to that was worse than any Apache torture to me. Well, that might be exaggerating if you've ever seen what those savages do to their captives. But it made me feel sick as a parrot. What was that girl playing at?

Seven

The Territory of New Mexico, a land of ragged peaks, parched deserts and grassy plains, was a place of vast distances over which travellers were carried by horseback, wagon train or stagecoach on rudimentary trails for in those late 1870s the Atchison and Topeka railroad had yet to creep over Raton Pass to Santa Fe. On the eastern side of the territory was the valley of the Pecos with its rich grazing lands. Its tributary, the Rio Hondo, ran down from the central mountains, the area of White Oaks, Fort Stanton and Lincoln. Over in the western sector, cutting down from north to south was the Rio Grande, which since the coming of the Conquistadores had served as a main thoroughfare, their Camino Real.

The trail past the Broken Back ranch wound through the mountains to connect with this route. Two weeks after the gunfight at White Oaks Alexandre Quiros announced that he was going to make a journey far south with a wagon-load of copper ore to the town of Mesilla in Dona Ana county on the banks of the Rio Grande. There he would meet a contact from across the border – he did not state specifically whether it was the Texan or Mexican border, which are both close by. The ore would be sold to this dealer.

'I'm leaving you, Shoot and Dan, to look after the ranch and the mine,' Quiros said, slapping my back. 'Belle's safety is in your hands.'

'Don't worry, I'll take care of her.'

Belle had been aloof and distant since we had got back from White Oaks. I would see her sitting on the veranda of their house when I came clopping in on my pinto after working out on the range all day. She appeared not to notice me and I was not invited over to play, either the guitar, or with her, again. Quiros seemed to suspect nothing of what had occurred. He must have had a touching faith in his wife's loyalty to leave her alone with me.

'I don't know what I'd do if anything happened to that gal,' he told me.

He had managed to put pressure on Colonel Dudley and wangle an escort of six troopers to accompany his wagon, for this journey south was the most dangerous in the Territory and entailed following the dreaded *Jornada del Muerto* before reaching the lush Mesilla valley. He would also be taking Shotgun Harry and Charley Bowdler along. It struck me as being a lot of protection for a single wagonload of copper but I guessed he preferred to be safe than sorry.

The Journey of Death was a 125-mile stretch of trail between the settlements of Socorro in the north and Dona Ana in the south without a single habitation in between. For ninety-five miles there was neither shade nor water. It had to be taken at a non-stop run to get through, for there was also the danger of imminent attack by Apaches and many a man had died on the trail. It was not a route I had travelled since the War nor did I care to try it again.

When the troopers had arrived and the wagon, heavily loaded, with a two-horse team, was ready to leave, I watched Quiros, his massive hams trembling, climb aboard, and the column set off as Belle stood in the shade on the veranda and waved goodbye. In a summer dress of white cotton she suddenly looked somehow delicate and vulnerable as, when they were gone, she stood alone. She did not look my way but went indoors. I was aching inside to touch her, for some sign from her.

'Right,' I muttered to myself. 'We'll see what's what.'

The Latino miners had already trooped off down into their shaft. It was early morning and Shoot and Dan planned to take the opportunity of venturing out on to Rudulph's land and rustling a few more strays.

'Count me out, boys. I'm sick.' I lay back on my bunk, groaning, holding my gut. 'It must be that muck George Washington served us up last night.'

'I'm OK,' Shoot said, brightly.

'Well, you're used to his pigswill. I'm not. You git goin'. I might catch you up.'

They exchanged glances but wandered off to saddle their broncs. I waited until I heard them going cantering off, then went outside. The sun was blazing down and it was deathly quiet, the only sound coming from the two Mex women-helps who were washing clothes at the tank. George Washington was in the cookhouse, probably asleep or getting drunk. It was just me and Belle!

My leather *chaparreras* were flapping, my spurs jingling, as I pulled my Stetson down over my eyes and headed over there, the twin Lightnings on my hips. I tapped on the kitchen door, but there was no reply. I rat-tatted more vigorously and Belle showed herself behind the net curtain in her white dress.

'Go away,' she ordered. 'I don't want to see you. Go back.'

'What the hell's the matter with you?' Anger surged through me and I smashed my gloved fist through a pane of glass, reached through, unlocked and shoved inside as she tried to hold me back.

'No,' she pleaded. 'Leave me alone. It's no good.'

Belle backed away to the kitchen table and snatched a kitchen knife. She was breathing heavily, her breasts almost bursting from the tight dress, her full lips half-opened, her speckled eyes fierce. 'Go away,' she screamed. 'I don't want you, Angel. Can't you see? You come any nearer I'll kill you.'

'Come on,' I coaxed. 'I'm not going to hurt you.'

'Yes, you are. There's no future in it for me. It's true what the sheriff said. You're a lousy 'breed, a cheat, a killer, a nobody, a fast gun, you'll be dead in a few years' time, if not before, or else in jail. You think I want

83

to get mixed up with you?'

This was not going to be easy. She was as vicious as a bobcat cornered up a tree, snarling at me. And her words stuck like barbed arrows in my heart. Maybe what she said was true, but I had to have her. 'You know you don't mean that, Belle,' I whispered as I closed in. For answer she slashed at me, but I caught her wrist, grabbed hold of her tight, and twisted the carving knife from her grip. She held her blonde-haloed head back from me, defiantly, panting from the struggle. 'It's no use, Belle,' I said. 'You're mine. And I'm yours.'

'No,' she protested, sobbing, as I gripped her in my arms. 'I don't want to be yours.'

For answer I swept her up in my arms and carried her into the bedroom, threw her on to the bed and, pausing only to remove my gloves, unbuckle my guns and jeans, as she stared at me, fell upon her. She was naked beneath the dress and groaned as I entered her. Whether it was a groan of pleasure or agony I wasn't sure.

We lay together drenched in sweat after our violent coupling, lay there a long time, Belle curled up in my arms. Suddenly I realized she was silently weeping, her tears wetting my shirt.

'What's wrong?' I asked.

'I'm frightened of what he'll do when he finds out. I know it will end badly. It's true what I said, Angel.'

'It ain't true. You want me. You know you do.'

Belle groaned and turned to cover me in a storm of kisses and we were off again. Actions spoke more than words. At noon we took a break for a bottle of cold French Chardonnay out of the well and some lunch, but stayed naked in bed. We dozed through the long siesta of the afternoon, and made love more gently.

When the boys came riding in, as the great red ball of fiery sun sank behind the fangs of the mountain range, I was sitting on the veranda, idly fingering my guitar.

Shoot reined in in a cloud of dust. 'You feelin' better? How's ya guts?'

'A lot better.' I flashed him an arrogant smile. 'Mrs Quiros gave me some of her medicine. She's sure got the healing touch.'

Later that evening, after they had eaten, when they heard me playing, the men drifted across, and the Mexicans began serenading us, even George Washington joining in with his deep booming voice.

Belle smiled and touched my knee. 'Wouldn't it be great,' she whispered, 'if it was like this every night.'

Yes, there was a sense of freedom and happiness between us with Quiros gone.

So as not to make things too obvious I wandered back to the bunkhouse with the men after we had said our goodnights. I needed the rest, anyhow.

Two or three days passed – I lost track of time. Most of it I spent in Belle's marital bed. Or, sometimes, we would hitch up the light buckboard and go for a drive. She didn't ride. But we would climb the rig to some look-out spot with a fine view and have a picnic. We were happy and laughing most of the time. But always there was an ominous sense of our time running out, of retribution hanging over me. Quiros, I figured, would be gone five or six days, but I couldn't be sure. He might be back any time. And what would happen then?

It was siesta time and we were just resting in Quiros's bed from an energetic and ex-perimental bout of sex when she murmured to me, 'It's true, we're made for each other, Angel. I've never known it like this before. What are we gonna do? I can't bear the thought of him touching me.'

'It didn't seem to worry you in that White Oaks hotel room.'

Belle paused and said, indignantly, 'I *am* his wife. I have to try to please him.'

'It sounded like a pretty good performance.'

'Maybe I was trying to make you jealous.'

'You certainly succeeded. I can't bear the thought of him touching you, either.'

'You! What about me? I'm the one who has to have his great blubbery weight on me, have him beside me all night. Don't you know how I hate that stench of bay rum in his greasy hair? Even the smell of his cigars nauseates me. I flinch every time he puts a finger on me.'

I stroked her hair and soothed her and she lay calm for a while before saying, 'You know I've had other men, don't you?'

'Well, I never thought you were as pure as the driven snow.'

'What was I to do? I came from a dirt-poor family. All I had were my looks. I worked the Mississippi river boats for a while, in the gaming saloons. There were a lot of fine gentlemen. I ended up in a sporting house in New Orleans. That's where I met Alexandre. He rescued me. He asked me to marry him. Oh, I liked him. He was witty and amusing and generous. He took me away from that awful life.'

'And brought you to this backwater?'

'Oh, it won't be for much longer. Once he's made his pile we're getting out. He's talking about going back to France, buying a chateau and estate someplace, living the life of a gentleman.'

'He must be wealthier than I thought,' I said, and noticed a bitterness in my voice. 'One minute you say you can't bear him, the next you sound like you're gittin' ready to emigrate. I don't understand you, gal.'

'Well,' she sat up away from me and reached for a bottle of white wine to refresh our glasses, revealing in the process a fine naked posterior, 'I bet you've had hundreds of little *queridas.*'

'Not hundreds. There've been a few.'

'An' I bet,' she mused, as she sipped the wine, 'once you've had your fun you get on your horse and ride out of there.'

'It's true. That's what I did, Belle. But this is different. I would never leave you. This is the real thing.'

'I bet that's what you say to all the gals. You're a typical *vaquero.* A sage rat. A saddle-tramp. How can I leave him for you?'

'I ain't going to be a saddle-tramp for ever. You and me, Belle, we could do well. We could be a team, go to Santa Fe, play the casinos.'

'He would follow you. He would kill you. And, probably, me too. He is a pretty neat shot, crafty and vicious. Or he would pay a bounty hunter to do it. We would never be safe.'

'I ain't scared of him.' But a chill passed through me for it was true, Quiros was a powerful and devious man to cross, I knew. 'I guess he's made some cash outa this copper mine.'

'It's not just copper. It's gold.'

'Gold?'

'Yes, there is copper. But deeper down there's a seam of gold.' Belle leaned back against the brass bedhead with a sheet across her, and bit her lip. 'Shoot! Why did I tell you that? Those Latino miners are terrified of him. He has sworn us all to secrecy.'

'I'm not surprised. If this gets out there'll be a stampede up here from White Oaks. Them miners will rip this land apart. So, the copper's just a cover? That's why he's taken the gold all the way down to the border, so nobody will know.'

'Yes, he sells it on to some Mexican *haciendado*.'

'Whoo!' I gave a whistle of awe. 'Your husband's getting rich.'

'Too true. Not that I see much of it. Sure, he buys me dresses and things. But he pays all the bills himself.'

'What about that big safe in there?'

'It's locked. He takes the key with him. You'd need to be an expert with dynamite to open it.'

'He's not stupid, our M'sieu Quiros.'

'You should have killed him when you had the chance.'

'What?'

'When he hit his head that night, that first night. You could have finished him. We could have made it look like an accident. We would have been free. You could have married me.'

'Are you crazy?' I turned to her, grabbed hold of her shoulders. 'I might kill men who take a shot at me. But I'm not a murderer.'

'You've got a psychopath's eyes. Ice-cold blue. You could do it, Angel.'

I considered this for moments. 'No. I ain't hanging, not even for you, gal.'

'Then, *what?* You think he won't find out about us?'

'Get your clothes on.'

'What?'

'There's one way out of this. Get dressed. We're leaving. Pack yourself a few dresses and things, but not too much. Hurry. We've no time to lose. We'll take the buggy. We'll go to Socorro and head north up the Rio Grande.'

'But, I can't ... not just like that.'

'Belle,' I cried, jumping out of bed, pulling on my jeans. 'You've forgotten what fun it is to be free, moving on each day. We can go where the hell we like. It's a wide country.'

'But–'

'Belle.' I extended my hand to her. 'It's me. Or him. Make up your mind.'

We told the Mex women to inform the boys we were taking a trip down to Lincoln for a couple of days, to throw them off the scent. We headed the buggy in the opposite direction, up over the pass and on towards the setting sun in its blood-streaked streamers of clouds. We drove the light rig all through the night as a great globe of moon rose high, flooding the mountain chasms with an eerie silver light. The Mescaleros, it was claimed, rarely attacked in darkness. They clung to their wickiups, fearing ghosts. Dawn was their time. Or, so we thought. But by then we had sighted the muddy, winding Rio Grande and the sun was rising again behind us, its rays flushing the box-shaped adobes of the old Latino town of Socorro a ruddy pink and purple.

Belle was exhausted from the night without sleep and insisted we book into the Socorro hotel for a few hours. I figured we had a day or two of grace before Quiros returned, the horse needed his rest and oats, too, so I didn't object too strongly, although I had a feeling we ought to get out of there as quickly as we could and head north for Santa Fe. I woke about noon in our room. Belle was in a deep sleep, so I didn't wake her. She had paid the hotel bill from a roll of greenbacks in her purse. It was all she had been able to scrape together. The little embroidered reticule was on the bedside table. Out of curiosity I carefully took a peep inside, counted the notes. There was seventy-five dollars. Maybe I could double it? That strange whirring sensation, the thumping in the chest, the butterflies in the stomach, the compulsion that draws a gambler as strong as an alcoholic's to drink, had hold of me. An inner voice warned me I was making a mistake, that I would regret this, but I could not resist. I tucked the wad in my shirt-pocket, buckled my gunbelts, tied my fancy bandanna and went downstairs.

The blast of noonday heat hit me as I stepped into the dusty street. A close and oppressive heat which intensified the stench of fly-buzzing rubbish piles, through which pigs grubbed, of sewage and cooking smells that pervaded the narrow streets. The main drag was rutted mud: there was little sign of movement or life, just a few listless nags at the hitching rails flicking their tails. Not a place to write home about. I pushed into the shade of a cantina and called for a tequila. The barkeep pushed a bottle and glass across. I took a bite of lemon, a lick of salt and swallowed a shot. Like in most Western towns the joint was already packed with men, mostly Latinos, some in the velveteens of *vaqueros*, hung with guns, others swarthy, scruffy peons in white cottons. A couple of card games were in progress.

A roulette table stood in the centre of the floor, and a croupier, flashily dressed, his face as sharp as a knife, set it spinning, luring me. '*Señor*, you wanna try your luck?'

'Sure, why not?' I ambled across and bought a handful of chips. Like all gamblers

93

I was filled with hope that this was going to be my lucky day. I would make myself a hundred dollars and repay Belle. I had a system. I placed my chips on the rouge and stuck to my lucky number as a couple of dark-faced hussies in torn and tattered dresses gathered around to urge me on. The ivory ball went bouncing merrily around and I had won. The girls screeched, and one clung on my arm. I knew she was longing to get her sticky little fingers on my winnings. So I played on. And again I won. This was too good to be true.

Yes, don't tell me. I should have stopped there and then while I had some dollars in the pot. It was too exciting, too enticing. Without realizing it I had practically emptied the tequila bottle and my head was spinning as fast as the wheel. With false bravado I gave the Mex harlots a lecherous grin, and tried again. Inevitably, I began to lose, and their faces fell, as no doubt did mine. An awful sense of panic gripped me for I knew the bottom was dropping out of my world. But I played wildly on.

'Place your bet, *señor*,' the croupier sang out.

I dug frantically in my pockets and came up with five crumpled dollars. 'No.' I shook my head. 'I've had enough.' I finished the tequila bottle and the girls drifted away when they saw there was no hope of a tip. I swallowed the last fiery drop in the glass and stumbled outside.

The sky had blackened over and suddenly there was an ominous crash of thunder and flashing blobs of lightning and the rain poured down. It was one of those summer storms that come from out of nowhere and are as suddenly gone. But this one was turning the main drag into a flood. I squelched along towards the livery intending to pay for the horse's keep with my last couple of dollars. The rain was hammering down, tipping from the brim of my hat. I had come out without a coat and my shirt was clinging to me. When I had settled up with the ostler, giving him three dollars, I had just two dollars left. In a stall at one side of the stable three ragged Mexican bums were down on their knees, crying out excitedly as they rolled dice. I couldn't resist. I could take these idiots. Wasn't I an expert at craps? Soon I was down on one knee shouting as loudly as them. To them, ten cents a throw was big stakes. And, at that time, it was to me.

'What the hell are you doing?' Belle was

standing there, wet hair hanging in strands over her face, the water running rivulets through her powder and paint, her dress sodden. 'Where's my money?'

Guiltily, I looked up. 'Hang on, honey, I'm winning.'

'Winning? Against these bozos? Big deal. I said, where's my cash? Don't tell me. You've lost it.'

'Don't start screaming, Belle. It ain't the end of everything.'

'Ain't it? I might have known. You damn drunken loser. You think I'm going to throw away everything I've got? You think I'm going to let you drag me down? You think I'm going back to this' – she spread her hands, her face anguished – 'this sort of life?'

I snatched up the fifty cents I had won, caught hold of the horse and buggy, and dragged it out into the rain. Belle was hurrying away, splashing through the puddles, her shoulders stooped. She screamed as she slipped in the mud and went flying. I caught up and tried to help her, but she thrust me away.

'Get on the rig,' I shouted.

She decided there was sense in that and, covered in mud, clambered up. I drove us back to the hotel through the streaming rain.

'What are you going to do?' I asked abjectly, as I watched her towel herself and begin to change into a dry dress. 'We could set off tonight for Albuquerque, and on to Santa Fe. Up there we can soon find ourselves some work.'

'Can *we*? Are you joking, Angel? Look in the mirror. Look at yourself. You should have stayed with those bums.'

'Oh, Chrissake.' My heart fell even further as I looked out of the window and saw half a dozen troopers splashing and jangling along the main street followed by Quiros, in his cape and big panama hat, driving an empty wagon, and Shotgun Harry and Charley Bowdler on horseback. 'It's them.'

Belle stood in her bodice and pantalettes, her eyes wide and distraught. 'Who?'

'Who you think? Your husband, that's who.'

Belle stood staring at me, her newly washed face losing all its colour. She looked as white as a ghost. 'What are we going to do?' she croaked out.

'Beats me.' Quiros had hauled in the wagon outside the cantina and, a man of massive girth, he climbed down and beckoned to the others. The troopers, Harry and Charley, followed him inside. 'They've gone into the saloon.' Without any cash in my pocket I was totally dispirited, in no mood to start out on the long drive north. 'Maybe,' I suggested, 'we could say you asked me to drive you over here on a shopping trip. Act innocent.'

'Perhaps.' She stood, brushing at her silver-blonde hair considering this. It was a ray of hope. And then it must have crossed her mind. 'What about the note?'

'What note?'

'The note I left on the kitchen table.'

'A note? Are you crazy?'

'I couldn't leave without saying something. He's been good to me. I just said I was sorry, I was going away with you, and not to follow us.'

'Oh, Jesus!' I grabbed my guitar and carbine. 'Quick. Pack your trunk. Get dressed. We've got to get back before he does. I'll take the buggy round the back. Hurry.'

I set the horse going as fast as I could, driving through the sucking mud out of Socorro, driving past the cantina, Belle holding up her parasol as a shield, both against the rain and the chance of being seen. Sodden and grimly unspeaking, we set the horse climbing back through the mountain passes, back the way we had come.

Eight

It was gone midnight by the time we reached the entrance to the Broken Back ranch. During the daylight hours we had kept a wary look-out for Mescaleros on the hilltops. But we had seen neither them nor travellers on the trail, nor stagecoach, nor wagoner, nor wandering panhandler. In fact, I regretted that this was so for, looking back in the moonlight, I saw our tracks clearly outlined on the muddy trail.

'That rain's done us a bad turn.' I hauled in, feverishly debating with myself whether to drive on past the ranch and leave the buggy some place. But, no, that would be foolish. I just wasn't thinking straight. 'Your husband ain't no fool. He's gonna see these tracks. Unmistakably a light rig, driving straight into here.'

We had barely conversed since leaving Socorro. 'So?' Belle asked. 'What are you in such a funk about?'

'Well, he's gonna put two and two together. What were we doing down in

Socorro? Maybe somebody recognized us there, too. And these Mex wimmin-helps here, maybe the men, they're gonna drop hints. People just love causing trouble.'

'So, what are you scared of? That he's gonna come gunnin' for you? You're supposed to be a fast draw. Can't you take him?'

'It's not just him. He'll have Shotgun Harry, Charley, Shoot, and the others behind him. I can't take 'em all.'

'You can try, can't you?' she asked, mockingly. 'Think of the prize. To the victor the spoils. Me, the ranch and the mine.'

'Very funny. You ain't got to fight four expert gunmen.' I urged the horse on into the ranch. 'I've had enough, Belle. I like life. I ain't throwing mine away. I'm taking the pinto and I'm getting out.'

'What about the seventy-five dollars you owe me?'

'Don't fret yourself. I'll send it to you some time.'

The ranch was in darkness except for one hurricane lamp. The dog they kept started barking. Shoot poked his head out of the bunkhouse. 'Who's there?' He was toting a revolver. 'Speak up or I'm gonna start shootin'.'

'It's all right,' I cried, wearily. 'It's us. Go back to bed.'

I pulled the rig in front of the ranch house.

'So,' she hissed. 'You're gonna run out on me like the louse you are? Don't you think that might make you look guilty?'

'What else can I do?'

'Tell the truth. So, we took a shopping-trip to Socorro? Sure, we were there. I can even say I freshened up at the hotel, if he's made enquiries. We didn't realize he had returned and came on back. Call his bluff.'

'You think he'll believe me?'

'That is for you to find out.' She grinned at me in the darkness before jumping down. 'It might be a good idea to keep your holster greased.'

'Yeah,' I agreed. 'OK, I'll put the rig away. I'll rub the hoss down.'

'I'm exhausted,' she said, stepping up in the ranch house door. 'I'm turning in. You know where the bunkhouse is.'

I watched her step inside, slam the door, and heard the key turn in the lock. 'Yes,' I muttered, 'I know my place.'

Quiros must have stayed overnight in Socorro because he didn't turn up until the next evening. All day I had been fidgety and nervous. I had gone out on the range, helping Shoot and Dan Coughlan to check and count the herd ready for the end-of-summer round-up when the full-grown beeves would be trailed into Fort Stanton or White Oaks for slaughter. We rode in at dusk and found that Quiros had not long arrived. The six cavalrymen had watered their horses, been given supper and were moving on back to the fort.

Quiros was calling out his thanks to them. He glowered at me and merely asked Shoot, 'Everything OK?'

'Sure,' the kid called across. 'You're back earlier than expected.'

'Yes. We made good time.'

He ignored me and lurched on up to the porch of his house, which made me wonder if he had his suspicions. After all, any of his lackeys left at the ranch must have had a good idea what was going on between me and Belle.

In the bunkhouse I had had to take some ribbing when I got in late the night before, little Jesus Guttierez looking across from his bunk, giving a whistle and saying, 'Hey, you been having a good time with the boss's wife, you lucky man?'

Shoot had joined in. 'I bet she's red hot, eh, Angel?'

And now Charley swaggered in in his leathers, long moustachios and battered hat, carbine in hand. 'Hey, I been thinkin' about you givin' it to her while he was away, you dirty ole ram.' He leered at me, slapping me on the back.

'Look,' I said to them all. 'Mrs Quiros and me git on fine an' I've driven her on a coupla shopping-trips. But that's all there is to it. She's the boss's wife and I'm the hired help. So don't go gettin' any other ideas.'

'Ha!' Charley slung his bedroll on his bunk. 'Who you tryin' to kid?'

'It's the truth. And anybody who says different in future is gonna have to answer to this.' I slapped my right-hand Lightning. 'You're slanderin' a fine lady an' I don't like that. Apart from that it can only cause trouble.'

'Waal,' Charley drawled. 'You would say that, wouldn't cha?'

'Trouble?' Dan Coughlan gave a scoffing, 'Ha! What you think you're asking for, Angel? I told you afore, that hellcat is best left well alone.'

'Yeah,' Charley agreed. 'Trouble's her middle name.'

'OK boys, you've had your say. There's nuthin' between me and Belle so let's drop

104

it, shall we?'

That seemed to quieten them, but I realized how easy it would be for one of them to drop a word to Quiros and stir him up.

A week passed in which I barely spoke to him or Belle. I kept my nose out of trouble and rode the sturdy little pinto out on the range. As we sat around our camp-fire Charley and Shoot spoke of making a raid on the Mescaleros and stealing some ponies, but I knew it was largely bravado. Although supposedly tamed by the army, the Messys were still lords of the vast, dark interior of the mountain range and anybody with any sense left them well alone.

On Sunday, the day of rest, I hung around the yard repairing some tack. I noticed Quiros go across to the mine-shaft with the mine foreman, Abe Klasner. He reappeared some time later, went into a huddle with the other miners, and started dishing them some cash. Jesus Guttierez seemed well pleased as he strolled over to me, stuffing greenbacks into his shirt-pocket. 'He OK, the boss.' It made me wonder just how good that gold-seam was down there? Maybe it was worth a fortune ... millions of dollars

... beyond a man's dreams?

Belle served her husband Sunday lunch on the veranda of their home and I could see he was polishing off a bottle of that cool, sparkling Chardonnay. Then he lay back on his hammock-swing in the shade, lit a cigar, and read a book. After a while he tossed it aside and waddled indoors to join Belle. I wondered, bitterly, if he was enjoying the kind of siesta I once enjoyed with her. To take my mind off them I joined in a game of cards for small change and, sometime later, heard the buckboard go clipping out. I took a look – Quiros was driving Belle, swerving out and along the trail. Maybe they were going for a picnic, the way we once did? How long, I wondered, could I stand this?

After supper I had a summons to go over and take my guitar. 'Who the hell he think I am?' I muttered to Shotgun Harry, who brought the message.

'You don't fool me, Alvorado,' he growled. 'You might fool the boss, but I weren't born yesterday.'

'Yeah, sure, and you could cause me big trouble. I've heard it before.'

'Hello there, Angel.' Quiros, dressed in a flowing white shirt with frilled cuffs and front, was the picture of bonhomie, waggling his cigar, offering me a glass. 'What are you going to play for us tonight? Belle loves your music.'

Yeah, I thought. I bet she does. 'Maybe I *should* be a *mariachi*. Do I get paid extra for entertaining your wife?'

'Ha!' he cried. 'You wouldn't be so mercenary, would you? Come on, take a chair, let's hear you.'

I played a couple of numbers without great enthusiasm, helped myself to the wine. It was dusk and the moths were attacking the hurricane lamp.

'You have a good trip?' I asked.

'Yes, excellent. And you, you took my wife into Socorro while I was away?'

'Yeah.' My heart gave a leap and I made out I was tuning my guitar to keep me cool. 'That's right. She said she wanted to do some shopping there. She's the boss so I obeyed.'

'It's strange that she should go so far. Didn't it occur to you that it could be dangerous?'

'Yes, that's why we drove overnight.'

'How long did you stay?'

'Not long. She said they didn't have what she needed. It started to pour, so we came back.'

'But you didn't drive back overnight?'

'Not all the way.'

'So, you put my wife's life in danger after I had trusted you to protect her?'

'What is this, a cross-examination? I thought I came here to play music?'

'It seems very strange to me.' He lit a cigar and in the light of the match I met his piercing black eyes fixed on me. 'Why should you go to Socorro to shop and not the more nearby White Oaks?'

'Beats me. Mine not to reason why. You better ask her.'

'And why should you leave Socorro in a great hurry the instant I and my party arrived?'

'I – I dunno – hey – we just left, thassal – we didn't see you – that's the truth.'

'You weren't aware that a party of half a dozen troopers had come into a quiet frontier town? You call that truth?'

'We left because *he* got drunk.' Belle had appeared catlike out of the night and was standing on the veranda behind us. 'Extremely drunk and offensive.'

'Offensive?' Quiros braced himself. 'You were offensive to my wife?'

'Aw, don't get het up, honey. You know his sort. As soon as they hit town they have to down a bottle of tequila. He just got on his high horse, saying he wasn't leaving and who was I to boss him around? Nothing to worry about. So I gave him the ultimatum, either drive me back or stay where he was. Yes, he drove me out of there in a hurry in that storm. But we didn't know you were there. I've told you that. Don't you believe me? What are you insinuating?'

'I leave you to guess at that.' Quiros splashed wine into his glass, spilling it, obviously upset. 'But understand, both of you, don't think you can pull the wool over my eyes.'

'What wool? What are you talking about?' Belle snapped. 'Have you dragged Angel over here to insult him? And me, too? What do you think we are?'

'I can only imagine,' he said, as he studied us, the cigar smoke curling. 'And it is not a very nice word.'

'Look, just what the hell are you accusing me of?' I got to my feet, my hands hovering over my guns. 'If you got anything to say, spit it out.'

'Angel, don't be a fool,' Belle warned, and went to sit on Quiros's lap, snaking an arm around his neck. 'Alexandre isn't accusing you of anything. He's just a silly old jealous thing, that's all.'

She nuzzled the fat man's jowls, tickling him, forcing him to smile. 'Why are you always like this to anybody who's nice to me, honey?'

Quiros laughed and hugged her. 'Sit down, Angel. I was just curious, that's all. Play us some more.'

Huffily, I resumed my chair. 'I ain't much in the mood.'

'Now, look what you've done, darling. You've made Angel sulk.'

'His month will be up next week,' Quiros remarked, as if I wasn't there. 'He says he'll be leaving. So, I guess it's *adios*, Angel.'

'Aw.' I strummed a few bars. 'I guess I could do another month. Just help you through the round-up and cattle-drive.'

'You will? That's mighty decent of you. And to show there's no ill will I'll give you a bonus. Let's up it to thirty a month. Only, don't tell the others.'

We pretended to talk about other things and I played and sang a few songs, but I could sense an underlying tension. Quiros was by no means convinced that my intentions were honourable. But, perhaps he had got used to men making passes at his wife.

'You seem young to claim to have been in

110

the war,' he remarked when Belle went inside to make some refreshments. Again it sounded as if he was calling me a liar.

'I was young. I ran away from home when I was fourteen and joined General Henry Sibley's force of nearly four thousand Texans when they came up the Rio Grande from Mesilla – the same way you came up the other day. There were about the same number of Union troops trying to stop us. It was early 'sixty-two. When we charged them across the river at Valverde they broke and ran. Us Confederates were expert horsemen and good shots while the Union boys were raw troops. Maybe you've heard of the Battle of Glorietta Pass?'

'Yes, but wasn't it indecisive?'

'You could say so. We were trying to take Santa Fe, fifteen miles further north. The Union had raised reinforcements and attacked us at Johnson's ranch in Apache Canyon. They hit our supply train, which hurt us as much as anything.'

'Couldn't you buy new supplies?'

'What, with Confederate dollars? Nobody wanted them. It was all retreating after Albuquerque was abandoned. Fighting and running, through terrible country, mountains and desert. We lost two thousand men

111

on that march back to San Antone.'

'So, after your somewhat inglorious war career what did you do? Anything of consequence?'

Belle had returned and was listening to her husband sarcastically grilling me, a slight smile on her lips.

'In 'sixty-five General Kirby Smith refused to accept the surrender and led two thousand men down into Mexico. I went with him and helped fight another war, that of General Juàrez against the French. Does that strike you as being of no consequence?'

'No. You helped rid Mexico of the hated French. So, what noble cause did you then espouse?'

'None, I'd had enough of causes. I took to wandering, as far west as the fabled Grand Canyon, as far north as Wyoming. Too cold for my liking, so I headed back to New Mexico. I've been stage-driver, gambler, wrangler, bull-whacker, and drover. Not much of consequence to you, I s'pose. The war's been over, what ... thirteen, fourteen years now and I've barely a cent to my name. Yes, I guess you're right, I'm just a sage-rat, saddle-bum, wandering cowboy, no-good *vaquero*. But, to tell you the truth, Mr Quiros, I'm happy with that. And I'd rather be me than you.'

'No need to get bitter, Angel,' Quiros laughed, 'but I guess I asked for that. Ah, the fount is dry. I must find us another bottle.'

When he lurched indoors in search of booze I grabbed hold of Belle's bare arm. 'I'll do it,' I hissed at her, angrily.

'What are you talking about?'

'You're right, Belle. We would be no good together on the trail, going nowhere, down-and-outs. We need all this, the mine, the cash. Then we'll be happy. We've got to have it, Belle. I'll think of a way. I'll get rid of him.'

'Shush.' Her eyes swivelled wildly. 'He's coming back.'

Quiros appeared with a bottle in each hand. 'Just what are you two talking about?'

'Nothing.' Belle shrugged. 'Angel's been telling me some more of his inconsequential adventures.'

'Yeah,' I grinned. 'So, folks, before I turn in, what do you want me to play for you? How about a nice funeral march.'

Nine

The dust raised by nearly a thousand head of cattle was enough to choke a man, and Quiros had put me to ride in the worst position – drag. You could feel the heat of the close-packed, boiling and bawling herd as we cracked our bullwhips and set them moving off the Broken Back range. We had only fifty miles to go to Fort Stanton but it would take the best part of three days, with two rivers to cross, the Bonito and the Ruidoso, the higher tributaries of the Rio Hondo. At least the herd would have water. Compared to the three-month hauls some Texas ranchers undertook to reach the railroads of Kansas this was small beer. But, as I kept my bandanna up high over my nose, my eyes half-closed, and, in my position at the rear end, yelled at the critters to get 'em moving, I knew that trouble could occur at any moment on a cattle trail.

Charley Bowdler and Dan Coughlan were riding flank, on either side of the beeves, while Shoot was up front at point. Quiros had decided to bring Belle along – leaving Shotgun Harry to protect the miners back at the Broken Back. Quiros and Belle were up ahead sitting beside George Washington on his chuck wagon.

The main danger, of course, is the chance of a sudden stampede. Wild longhorns don't like being taken where they don't want to go. Sometimes it seems they know they're gonna end up as minced beef and will do anything to get out of there. The slightest thing can spook 'em, the flare of a match as a man lights a cigarette, or any sudden noise or movement, and they're off. Sometimes it's not accidental. Plenty of herds have been stampeded by rustlers. And there was no shortage of badhats and desperadoes in New Mexico Territory.

We had spent three weeks rounding up and cutting out the full-grown beeves, and close work with longhorns is never easy. One swing of those arrow-sharp great horns by an angry bull who means business can take out a man's leg. Fortunately, my tough little cream-and-dun paint was a good cow-horse and could swerve and turn on a five-cent piece. We built a makeshift chute to rebrand the big un's. There would be no bulldogging *them*. It was easier to poke them into the cage, push the hot iron through the bars into their sides and turn them loose.

As the herd grew in size we had to stay out on the range to keep them in one place. So I hadn't seen much of Belle, and I was feeling as horny and hard done by as any of those angry bulls. When we watered the herd the first night at the prearranged spot, Quiros already had a tent set up on the bank of the stream and Belle was sat on a camp chair. She was decked out in a low-cut cotton dress of blue, with puffed sleeves, brushing at her blonde hair, and looked like she was out on some Sunday picnic. She gave no indication that she had even noticed me. I brushed the dust from my clothes and went to dunk my head and cool my throat in the water.

The herd was content enough spread out alongside the river, so Quiros set Shoot and Dan to watch them while the rest of us ate. After that blazing day even George Washington's chilli Colorado and beans, red hot as it was, tasted good. Charley and I eased our bones, lay out against our saddles, and watched the sky turn from flaming orange to orchid-purple shades as the sun dropped behind the dark ridge of hills. He made cigarillos from black tobacco rolled in corn husks and passed me one; we lit them with straws.

'Seems mighty peaceful, don't it?' He grinned.

'Maybe,' I said, 'it's the lull before the storm.'

I strummed my guitar, picked out the tune of *'The Streets of Laredo'* and began softly singing, 'Play the fifes lowly ... beat the drums slowly ... play the dead march as you carry me along...'

'You've a very mournful taste in music,' Quiros shouted across at me. 'But I guess it soothes the cattle.'

He came and perched on a log on the other side of the fire, warming himself, and Belle nestled down in a shawl by his feet, resting her back against it. Her dress was partly hitched up and I could see the curve of her calf. Just the sight of it inflamed me more than if she had been sitting there stark naked.

'How about this one?' I called. 'Oh, Western wind when wilt thou blow ... so the black clouds down will rain. Christ, that my love were in my arms ... and I in her bed again.'

Belle smiled and licked her upper lip with

her pink tongue-tip, her eyes meeting mine. But Quiros called out, 'Yeah, OK, cowboy. Maybe you'd better go back to caterwauling in Spanish.'

'What's the matter? Don't you like the lyrics?' I had grown tired of his patronizing airs, always rubbing it in that he was the big boss and I was the penniless employee, who, in spite of all efforts had never gotten anywhere. So I teased him with another high-pitched refrain:

'Eyes like the twinklin' stars,
Cheeks like a rose,
Belle is a pretty girl,
God Almighty knows.'

Quiros adjusted his portly frame, searched for his leather cigar-case in a pocket of his caped greatcoat.

'Don't push your luck, Angel.'

'My luck? What would you know about my luck, Mr Quiros?'

He lit up and sucked at the thick green Havana. 'Well, by the look of those worn-out boots you ain't never had much. And if you ain't careful it could run out altogether.'

'Sure,' I drawled, putting the guitar aside and wrapping my blanket around my legs, lying back on the saddle. 'Time to git me some shut-eye. Wake me at midnight for the funeral watch. I don't suppose you'll be taking a turn, will you, Mr Quiros?'

I didn't wait for his reply, but pulled my hand down over my nose and tried to forget them. What was I doing, getting drawn into this fool relationship, anyhow? But I could not ignore Belle. Her nearness nagged at me like a boot on a raw heel.

Exhaustion finally made me drift off into sleep. When I woke they had gone, no doubt retired to their tent. The stars told me it was near midnight. Time to go relieve Shoot and Dan. Charley was snoring, his mouth open, blowing through his hairy moustache. Aw, I thought, let him sleep. I picked up my carbine and went to pick out a spare mustang from the remuda to give the pinto a rest. As I did so something or someone stirred the bushes nearby. I swung to cover them with the Winchester and the moon-light outlined Belle's shape through the blue cotton dress, shining on her hair like pale gold. I caught her in my arms, pushing her back against a tree, sinking into her wonderful softness, biting hungrily at her lips.

'I've missed you,' she gasped. 'I need you so much.'

Like most of our 'lovemaking' it was hot,

harsh and hurried. Did love come into it? Or was it pure, frantic lust?

'I can't bear being apart from you,' Belle moaned, as we floated down, back into sanity, in the aftermath. 'When are you going to do it?'

'Do what?'

'Kill him.'

Her blunt words certainly brought me back to cold reality. 'I've got to wait my chance. I've got to fix it so it doesn't throw any suspicion on us.'

'Do it soon,' she hissed, 'or I'll get somebody else to.'

'That would be a fool thing to do and you know it.'

'Hold me,' she begged. 'Hold me tight for a bit. When we're married, you'll never leave me, will you?'

'Nope. Why should I want to do that?'

'I know you *vaqueros*. I had better get back. I crept out while he was sleeping, but he might waken. Do it soon, Angel.'

'I will. Don't you worry, Belle. That man has only a short time left on this earth.'

Suddenly I heard someone blundering through the undergrowth towards us. I grabbed for one of my .38s but released pressure on the trigger. It was Charley.

120

'Hey!' He grinned from ear to ear beneath his moustachios. 'Ain't you the sly ones?'

'Pipe down, will ya?' I released Belle's hand and she slipped away back to her tent. 'It ain't what you think. She came out to attend to the call of nature. I bumped into her.'

'Yeah, tell me another.'

'Come on.' I swung on to my mustang. 'Those boys will be wondering where we are.'

Dawn lightened the sky as we were warming ourselves with a well-earned tin mug of black coffee around the camp-fire when suddenly Pete Rudulph and a dozen men rode in. They were a pretty ominous-looking bunch, reining in, sitting their broncs, carbines and rifles laid across the horses' necks, ready to use.

'To what do we owe this pleasure?' Alexandre Quiros was standing in a flowing nightshirt that did little to disguise his bulk. Even at this early hour he was puffing on a cigar. I had to admire his nonchalant attitude under duress, I'll give him that. He didn't scare easy. 'Out early, aren't you, Mr Rudulph?'

Rudulph, a scrawny, grey-bearded patriarch, a sharp prow of nose jutting from beneath his hatbrim, said in an indignant, quavering voice, 'We rode all night to catch up with ye. We need to take a look at these brands.'

'Really, and why should that be?'

'Because I been losing a lot of stock from my range and I believe these dang-blasted sons of bitches you employ are to blame. I'm sorry, ma'am' – he touched his hat to Belle – 'but I have strong emotions about this.'

'You're suggesting that some of my herd might be stolen stock?'

'I wanna take a look at the brands, thassall, just to check they weren't originally Barbed Y beeves.'

'Well, Mr Rudulph, you always get a few mavericks and if you find any which might be regarded as yours you are welcome to take them back. But I fear you're barking up the wrong tree. This herd belongs to me. I trust my men implicitly.'

'Huh!' Rudulph gave a loud and doubtful sound. 'We'll see about that. Come on, boys. Let's take a look.'

'Look all you like.' Quiros watched the riders move on and manoeuvre through the big herd, bending over to study the brands. 'Don't let those trigger-fingers get itchy, men. There's too many of 'em for us. Come on, Washington, that bacon smells good. Let's be having some.'

When the riders came jogging back in he was sat on his log munching at a great plateful of bacon and beans.

'So what's the news, Mr Rudulph? You found any belonging to you?'

'A few.' Rudulph spat in the dust, sighed, and looked around at us. 'Not enough worth botherin' about.'

'Good. Why don't you step down and join us?'

Old man Rudulph's nose twitched at the aroma of bacon and coffee and he looked like he'd sorely like to, but pride prevented it. 'I'm just warning you, Mr Quiros, if you employ scum of the earth like these you better expect trouble.'

'Harsh words, Mr Rudulph.'

'I tell you the truth. If we ever catch these lowdown filthy rustlers red-handed there's goin' to be killing.'

We were speechless for moments as Rudulph wheeled his horse away and his men began to follow. Then Charley Bowdler called out, 'You ever call me scum of the earth again, Rudulph, you better be ready to face me.'

'Me, too,' I said, backing away, loosening my self-cockers in their holsters.

'Yeah, an' me.' Shoot raised his carbine, while Dan Coughlan just stood there looking his usual dour self, a saddle gun in one hand.

'Boys, don't let's get iffy.' Quiros got to his feet and fluttered his fingers, trying to placate us. He knew the code: men like us didn't take insults like that, however true, from anybody, never mind the odds. '*If* you say this, *if* you say that. Mr Rudulph has not found anything to legally complain about. And I need you to get this herd on the move. You're no good to me dead. So, let's breakfast, shall we, and say *au 'voir.*'

Even Rudulph had to grin at his quaint, high-pitched manner of speaking. It somehow took the tension off what might have been, if released, a bloodbath. 'You been warned,' was all he said before he led his men trooping away.

Twenty dollars a head! That was the price I overheard Colonel Dudley at Fort Stanton agree to pay. The army needed meat to feed its men and there was an agreement to supply beef to the Indian reservation, too. The army didn't quibble about spending the taxpayers' cash. Dudley signed a cheque for payment at Quiros's Lincoln bank. Twenty times a thousand? My basic arithmetic was a bit shaky, but I struggled with the figures. Twenty thousand dollars? Had I got that right? Jeeze! That was a hell of a lot of cash.

The pompous colonel was getting redder than usual around the gills as Quiros pocketed the cheque, but appeared to be arguing with him. 'No,' I heard Dudley say, 'we cannot countenance giving you another military escort for a single wagon. We have more pressing things to do. If you wish to make such a dangerous trip again you do so at your own risk.'

Quiros looked disgruntled but pumped the colonel's hand, smoothing troubled waters, as usual.

'What was all that about?' Belle asked.

'Oh, I have to take another consignment of copper down to Mesilla. He's refused to give us an escort. Still, I'm sure my scum-of-the-earth fast guns can protect me.' He smiled at Charley and me. 'We'll be leaving on Wednesday. You two, Dan and Shoot, can come along. Darling, I'll leave Harry to protect you. You'll be all right. Hopefully, this will be my last run.'

You can say that again, I thought. He had

played right into my hands.

'Come on,' Quiros took my arm. 'Let's get out of here before they start smashing their axes into these poor critters' skulls. Their terror and moaning upsets Belle.'

How odd, I thought, as we mounted up and rode off, that he should be so concerned about the tender feelings of a woman who wanted him dead.

We stopped off in White Oaks. George Washington needed to stock up on beans and Belle wished to collect her new green velvet dress.

'Boys, I'm giving you a bonus,' Quiros said, handing us ten dollars each. 'You've earned it.'

The boys were happy enough with the unexpected cash and quickly began to drink it away at the Claremont bar.

'You know how much he made?' I asked Charley as we sank tankards of German steam beer. 'Twenty thou. And he gave us ten dollars each.'

Charley Bowdler's muddy eyes in their narrow slits hardened as he looked at me over the top of his glass. 'Twenty thousand? Ain't there any way we can relieve him of that?'

'No. It's a cheque payable to his bank.

126

But, if we're going down to Mesilla with him there might be a way of rearranging his assets more equitably. Would you be interested?'

'What you mean?' Charley grunted. 'Kill him?'

'Possibly. Would you be with me?'

'Sure, why not? Twenty thou. Wow!'

'How about Shoot and Dan?'

'They do what I tell them. But, what's the good? He'll only be carrying copper. There's no money in that.'

'He'll be carrying gold.'

'Gold?'

'Yes. He fences it off to some Mexican.'

'Gold? Not copper? I see.' Charley tugged at his danglers, his face lighting up. 'Count us in. I've had enough of working for peanuts.'

Ten

Six days later we set off from the Broken Back mine escorting a wagon carrying, we believed, sacks of gold beneath the copper ore. At Socorro Quiros put fresh horses in the shafts, two of them, and roped a barrel of water to the wagon, to sustain us over the long barren stretch south to Mesilla: the Journey of Death. We set off at a jog-trot, Quiros driving, while I sat beside him on the box, my Winchester primed. It was a long, empty trail, a rutted dirt-track winding across tawny plains and down rugged red-rock chasms, ideal ambush spots for Apache. On and on we went through scabland and slope country and as the sun sank it seemed to burn a hole through the shirt on my back.

'Don't come back unless it's done,' Belle had hissed at me before we set off. 'I can't go on like this, Angel.'

I had nodded, grim-faced, at her from my perch on the wagon as we set off in the hard orange dawn. She stood on the veranda of the house, Shotgun Harry and the miners in the dusty yard, watching us go.

'We must have put forty miles between us and Socorro,' Quiros called out towards the end of the day. 'We'll pull into the shelter of this rock and rest the horses. We'll set off again at midnight, boys.'

None of us spoke. We didn't have a lot to say. We were edgy, for it lay heavy on us, the thought of what we had to do. Or, at least, it did on me.

'We come a fair piece,' I agreed, finally, as I hunkered down to light a small fire and boil up coffee. 'You figure we'll make Mesilla by tomorrow night?'

'With any luck, if we take it steady.' The fat man sat on a rock and dosed himself with a slug of brandy. His paunchy face was wreathed with dust and his canvas suit was red instead of white, the same as us all. His fierce black eyes were uneasy as they darted hither and thither watching Shoot watering the horses, Dan opening a sack to give them handfuls of split grain, and Charley taking a piss. 'Pass it round.'

He palmed the cork back in the bottle, tossed it across. My Adam's apple jerked as I took a couple of good swallows. I stuck the cork back in and tossed it to Charley.

'Hey, real French brandy,' Shoot whooped, snatching it eagerly after Charley had supped.

'The best,' Quiros said. 'Hey, boys, leave a drop more for me.'

'Here.' Dan took it from Shoot. 'Let a man have a drink.' He tipped the bottle and the fiery liquid glugged down his throat. We watched, amused, as he drank on. The bottle was perpendicular now. 'Ah,' Dan gasped, as he wiped his thumb across his mouth. 'That's better.'

Quiros caught the bottle as it was tossed back to him – empty. 'You greedy bastard.'

The hard-faced Dan Coughlan swung towards him, his eyes glinting under his hat band. 'What did you call me? That was a slander on my mammy.'

'Get lost. You should remember who you're talking to. I pay your wages.' Quiros pointed a finger at the sullen man. 'I hire you.'

Shoot caught my eye and began to back away from the water-butt out of the line of fire, his fist closing over the butt of his .45. I raised myself from the fire and pushed a horse out of the way. I wasn't ready for this.

'Not much longer you don't,' Dan drawled, turning his back to Quiros and secretly easing a sawn-off shotgun from the saddle holster. He cocked it with a thumb and swung back, firing from the waist. Blam!

But he was too late. With remarkable speed Quiros anticipated what was happening and whipped a snub-nosed 'Storekeeper' from his pocket; the shot thudded into Dan's chest. He was catapulted back, his buckshot nearly peppering us instead.

'Anybody else?' Quiros asked in his high-pitched voice. He was perched on his rock like a cornered animal and looked around at us, waving the gun in a semicircle as he recocked it.

'Yes, me,' Shoot shouted and he jerked out his long-barrelled old Colt Frontier. 'He was my pal.'

Quiros sent the empty bottle spinning at the boy's head, which made him flinch and lose his momentum. Too bad for him. The Storekeeper blazed and Shoot went down clutching his gut.

'Hell,' I muttered.

This wasn't on my agenda. I had been planning to jump the big man later. My Lightnings were still in their holsters, my hands hanging over them as Quiros pointed the stubby revolver my way and asked,

'Well, are you going for it, too, Angel?'

'No, *I* am,' Charley bellowed, before I could decide one way or the other.

With amazing speed for a fat man Quiros rolled from his rock and came up shooting. Charley was too fast for him. His stolen Remington revolver belched flame and lead, smashing into Quiros's chest.

The Frenchman groaned and rolled over, staring up, pleadingly, at me. 'Angel...?'

'Don't worry, I'll look after Belle. And your mine,' I said. 'By the way, this was her idea.'

Quiros gritted his teeth as he tried to raise his smoking gun. 'You filthy rotten–'

I didn't hear what he was going to call us because Charley's Remington crashed out again and a slug between the eyes finished him. The fat Frenchman lay there, lifeless eyes staring at me.

'Well.' My Lightnings were still in my holsters. I breathed a sigh of relief. 'What a mess. I didn't know you boys were planning to act so fast.'

Charley stood there in his battered hat and torn chaps, his stars-and-stripes bandanna, his mad eyes fixed on me, as was the deathly eye of his solid-framed Remington. 'Now it's jest you an' me, ain't it, Angel?'

I was transfixed by his stare for seconds, like a rat before a rattler. And then I drawled, 'You, and me and the Apaches. There's one up there on that rock behind you. He's got an arrow fixed on your back.'

If he had turned to look I would have gone for him with my guns, but he just cackled. 'Don't try that ol' trick, Angel.' He grinned at me. 'What I was sayin' was it's jest you an' me to share this gold.'

'Sure. But if there are Messys about they will have heard them gunshots five miles away. We gonna need each other's help to get outa here.'

'Right, boy.' Charley holstered the Remington. 'That's true.' He shook his head and tugged at his moustachios. 'Look at poor ol' Shoot and Dan. They're done fer. I weren't expectin' this, neither. I thought Dan could take him. Look at that fat Frenchie. He moved damn fast.' He poked at Quiros with his boot and bent down to go through his pockets. He took watch, cigar-case, wallet stuffed with a wad of greenbacks, and tossed away other bits and pieces of no use to him, not offering to share the spoils with me.

I didn't mind. I was going for bigger game and I was shocked by the sudden demise of

133

Alexandre Quiros, a man who, in some ways, I had half admired. A line of ants was heading for a pool of blood that was fast seeping from him.

'What a way to go,' I breathed out, 'a man with all his talent and ability.'

'He shouldn't have been so damn greedy, should he?' Charley went through Dan's and Shoot's pockets, too. 'I believe in fair shares.'

'So I see,' I muttered.

'What shall we do with 'em? Toss 'em off the cliff?'

'No. We'll leave 'em where they are. But first...' I went over to the wagon. When Quiros wasn't looking I had secreted a lance and an arrow taken from the fight with the Mescaleros as souvenirs. I took them out and stuck the lance hard into Quiros's belly. It went in making a sucking sound. I thudded the arrow in Shoot's chest. 'It'll look like the Apaches did it.'

'How about the bullet holes?'

'Apaches have got guns, ain't they?'

'Yeah, some have, too true.' He eased the Storekeeper from Quiros's tightening grip and took the Frontier from Shoot, hurling them into the rocks. 'Now nobody's be able to work out who shot who.'

'Come on, let's get the hosses harnessed and hit the road.'

'Yeah, this place gives me the creeps.'

'We'll drive all night and rest up at dawn.'

'Good thinkin' Angel.' He gave a rousing whoop, strutting like a turkey-cock. 'Hey, man, you realise somethang? We're rich.'

'Yeah, let's take a look at that gold.' I pulled the tarpaulin away from the wagon and hauled aside the sacks of copper. Underneath lay sacks which, when we split them open, revealed glistening lumps of gold ore. 'Whoo! We sure are rich. We'll sell this lot to that fella down in Mesilla and have us a high old time, Charley.'

He slapped my back. 'We sure will, pardner.'

So my plan had succeeded beyond my wildest dreams. Quiros was dead and I hadn't had to fire a shot. Nobody could hang *me*. Soon I would be a rich man, married to a beautiful wife, owner of a ranch and mine. My future looked rosy. My only problem now would be to deal with Charley and Shotgun Harry. Both hard men. But I believed I could handle them. To tell the truth, I felt like nothing could stop me.

How little did I know.

Charley Bowdler was as cocky as a rooster soon as we reached Mesilla. The fertile, river-watered fields thereabouts had attracted a good few settlers to farm, both Mex and Anglo, and raise livestock, market their fruit, corn and vegetables. But the old town of Mesilla, with its boxy 'dobes, rain-lashed holes in their walls, a tattered skin hanging to serve as a door, was still the hard-bitten and rumbustious place where anything went. Close to the frontier, it har-boured numerous *bandidos* and smugglers dealing in contraband, guns, stolen girls, and yes, gold.

And to service their lusts and thirsts and love of gambling many cantinas and saloons had sprung up, their plank false fronts proclaiming, 'Eldorado', 'Rainbow's End', 'Dirty Martha's', 'Hank's Hotel', or 'Hell's Kitchen'.

Bowdler, the killing of Quiros proud inside him, gold and greenbacks stuffed in his pockets, swaggered along the shady sidewalks, his thighs wide, as if he'd got a grocer's weight swinging between them. He kicked his high-heeled boots to make his spurs jangle-jingle, whooped and crowed, and gave jumps of crazy-assed elation. Folks

136

stepped back to let us pass and I didn't blame 'em.

'Hey, let's hit the Eldorado,' he yelled, digging a bony elbow in my midriff. 'I wanna tangle my legs with a few of them easy gals.'

The Eldorado was the flashiest of all the joints with a real mahogany bar and mirrors behind the shelf of bottles, all imported overland by bull-trail. It even had a big chandelier of fifty-candle-power suspended from the ceiling. It had formerly been an old Spanish mansion and was the most solid place in town, its adobe walls three feet thick. That made it cool and well protected, so before we pushed through its swing doors we weren't ready for the crash of sound that greeted us. Men were three deep along the bar, drinking as if there was no tomorrow, girls in skimpy lace dresses whooping and wheeling on the stage, as a Mexican *mariachi* band pumped out a noisy number. The Wheel of Fortune was spinning, a gang of gamblers grouped around it, and, under the sign of the tiger, a faro game was in progress.

'Hey,' Charley yelled, scooping a passing waitress into him. 'This really is Paradise.'

'Don't talk so soon,' I shouted through the

137

din at him. 'Before you go getting liquored-up I think we oughta go see the sheriff of this town and sort out our story 'bout what happened.'

'Hey, cain't you see, I'm busy?' Charley licked a lecherous tongue up the cheek of the little dark-eyed *querida* in his arms, and with the other reached out to grab a bottle of rum that came sliding along the bar to him. 'You go see the damn sheriff.'

'OK. But the story is we were attacked by the Messys, who killed the boss and t'others. We beat 'em off and got away. We stick to that if anybody asks.'

'Yeah, yeah.' Charley already had his nose deep in his tumbler of liquor or the *querida*'s bosom. 'You tell him that. That's what happened fer Chrissakes, ain't it?'

'Yeah, but there's no need going throwing greenbacks and gold around like it's your last day on earth. We don't want to draw attention to ourselves.'

'Arr, you worry too much, *amigo.*' Charley put up a filthy hand and pushed it in my face, shoving me away. 'Less go fer it.' He tossed a handful of Quiros's greenbacks fluttering along the bar and shouted for drinks for the whole saloon. 'You still here, Angel?'

'Take it easy, Charley.'

But it was as much good as telling a bull who came racing and bucking out of the chute at a rodeo to take it easy. Charley was intent on drinking the town dry and painting it red.

By then we had conducted our business with the Mexican landowner, or bigshot from over the border. As we rolled our wagon into town, the spare horses tied behind, we had spotted him, in his silver decorated costume and huge sombrero, sitting on a chair in the shade of the canopied sidewalk. There was a gang of villainous-looking *vaqueros* sprawled nearby. 'That's him,' Charley hissed, recognizing the *hombre* from his previous visit with Quiros.

'Leave this to me.' I was standing on the foot-brake and bringing our exhausted team to a halt beside the big chief. 'Howdy,' I called. 'Would you be waiting for us?'

'Where's Señor Quiros?' he asked in Spanish, lighting a thin cigar. 'Who are you?'

'He got delayed. I'm his top man. You interested in this cargo of copper or not? Otherwise we'll go on and sell it down in El Paso.'

'You will do no such thing, young man.'

The *haciendado* got to his feet with a jingle of silver conchos hanging from his sombrero-brim and looked under the tarpaulin. 'The same amount of copper, is it? The same price you want?'

'That's what he told me. I'm only his messenger-boy. You can keep the damn wagon, too.'

'Give him my thanks.' The old man, gold teeth glinting in the dark planes of his face, gave a nod to one of his men, who picked up two gunny sacks, which appeared to be of considerable weight, and swung them up to me. I caught them and passed one to Charley. I peered inside and saw gold and silver Peso coins. Who cared if they were not dollars? This was the language of the frontier. The *lingua franca,* I believe they say. The *haciendado* was grinning up at me. 'OK, *muchacho?* You send message and we meet again.'

'What you think Charley? This fair trade?'

'Hell! It's good enough fer me. Who's got time to count it? You keep yourn, Angel. As for me I'm gonna spend, spend, spend.'

'Before you do that,' I suggested, as he jumped down from the wagon, 'I think we oughta stash this in the hotel room. Then we go out and have our fun. It's a lot of moolah.'

I tipped my hat to the fancy-dressed *haciendado* and drawled, 'See you next time, *señor.*' Fortunately, Charley was sober at that time and saw sense in what I said. We booked separate rooms at a joint called Hotel Grotti, extracted some spending money from the heavy sacks of pesos, locked our doors, and went to take a look at the town.

That was late afternoon. Now it was dusk. I left Charley to wallow in booze, cigars and women, as much as he could possibly take of each, in noise and excitement, and went out into the street. Slapping some of the dust from my clothes I went in search of the local lawman.

'Jailhouse', the sign read. 'Law Enforcement Officer.' Pedro Borrero had his boot-heels up on his desk, a carbine propped alongside. He was fat and sweaty and fanned himself with a dirty newspaper as I stepped inside. '*Si*, wha' you wan'?'

I briefed him on what had happened, trying to seem suitably shocked. Our wagon-load of copper attacked by Mescaleros. My boss, Señor Quiros, and two men killed. We, me and my pal, Charley, had made a run for it in the wagon and escaped.

'Where ees your friend Charley? I need

141

verify your story.'

'He's gettin' pisscalated. Man needs a drink after an experience like that.'

'Thees 'pache, how they keel your boss?'

'They hit us with arrows, lances and guns as we stopped for a break. We were just lighting a fire. We didn't have a prayer.'

Pedro stared at me, picking at his teeth with a match and pushed a bottle of tequila across, followed by a glass. 'You still got wagon?'

'No, as soon as we got in we were approached by some Mexicans, Señor Quiros's regular contacts, who offered us cash for it. I figured it best to get rid of it and take the proceeds back to Quiros's widow. She's gonna be needing it. Unfortunately, my pal, Charley Bowdler, decided to take half the proceeds and he's in the process of going through that cash now like greased lightning.'

'Bowdler? I hear of heem. Bad man, rustler. How come you with heem?'

'Well, you know, these parts you get who you can to work for you. Señor Quiros hired him. He seems honest enough. He just wants to have a good time, thassall.'

'*Sí*, don' we all.' Pedro yawned and scratched himself as I took another glass of tequila. I felt like getting drunk myself. 'I will try to raise posse, go out, take look at these bodies, by the big rock shaped like sombrero, you say?'

'Yeah, you can't miss it. You goin' now?'

'Hey, no. *Mañana* will do. Have anudder dreenk.'

I did. I had an idea that in Pedro's book *mañana* never came.

Eleven

My mind spinning with the events that had occurred, I had a few more drinks in the Eldorado and tried my hand at faro. Instead of a guy running the game there was a girl, Rafaela, slim and brown in a flame-coloured off-the-shoulder gown, smoking factory-rolled cigarettes, a mane of shining black curls rolling down across her shoulders. It's a simple frontier game of chance and – without boring you with the rules – or ways of bending the rules – it resolved itself into a simple matter of betting any card to win or lose. The player – or sucker – generally had an even break, which accounted for its popularity. Most men were tired of being rooked by gambler dudes in some crooked poker-game, or of trying to buck the roulette wheel with its 36-to-1 or the added zero or double zero. Faro was even-Steven, as they say. Or an idiot's game.

Was that why I was winning? No; Rafaela, sitting at the head of the table below the big coloured sign of the Bengal tiger, was shuffling the cards and clicking them out of the case-box abacus after bets had been placed on the lay-out. In a terminally bored voice she sang out, 'Loser', or 'Player', and pushed a pile of chips equivalent to the bet the winner's way. Funnily enough, now I was rich and really didn't give a damn, more of these were coming my way. I met Rafaela's liquid eyes and she smiled and pushed some more cash across. You know, I had the feeling I'd clicked.

There was no sign of Charley Bowdler but about 4 a.m. he came stomping into his room next to mine and crashed on to the bed. All I heard after that was him being sick on the floor and then his hearty snores. It crossed my mind to go in there, slit his throat, take the sack of pesos, and wish Charley goodbye. But I never like making things too obvious.

At noon I breakfasted, soaked in a tub in the Chinese bath-house, and had a body massage from an almond-eyed gal, while I sent out for some new duds. I came out of there smelling of strange perfume, my muscles tingling, and decked out in velveteen pants, a new pair of snakeskin boots with solid silver toes, a flounced white shirt and leather jacket. Around my hips were slung my trusty Lightnings. And I had a new black hat on my head, its brim rolled high on each side like crow's wings. The only original article of wear I retained was Belle's lavender bandanna.

Mid-afternoon Charley rolled in like a sailor in a force-ten gale, his splayed legs rolling. I could tell from his glazed expression he had the biggest hangover a man had ever known. He reinforced this by coiling himself over the bar and pressing an iced glass of steam beer to his forehead.

'Howdy, Charley,' I said. 'Have a good night?'

He groaned by way of reply. 'Where you been? You smell like a Turkish brothel.'

'*Sí*, and you still stink like a *vaquero*. Charley, I been thinkin', it's time we split.'

'Split?'

'Yes, you go your way and I go mine.'

His mahogany-dark face suddenly tensed as hard as saddle leather, and his eyes flickered like a snake's in their slits. His neat nostrils literally flared as he snarled at me, 'You ain't goin' nowhere without me. I'm your shadow. You better git used to that.'

'What you talkin' about, Charley? Look, you agreed to do this job for gold at the end of it. You've done it and you've got your gold. About two thousand dollars of it. That ain't nuthin' to sneeze at.' I had counted out my sackful that morning on the bed and I figured his about equivalent. 'That's a good pay-out. Now you and me, it would be safer if we split. The lawman's started asking questions.'

'Yeah? Listen, *hombre*, don't think you can scare me away. I tell ya, I'm sticking with you. I'm coming back to the Broken Back mine with you. You're going to marry that red-hot bitch and I'm gonna be your ramrodder. Every consignment of gold you bring outa that mine you're gonna split fifty-fifty with me.'

'No, I don't think so. That wasn't in the deal.'

'Come on, Angel.' He tried to put his arm around me. 'You and me, we're pardners. Thass the way it's gonna stay. Fifty-fifty. Everything you get, I get. Or that lawman really is going to start asking questions. You an' your bride-to-be arranged all this. You fancy kicking air on the end of a rope along side Belle, Angel? Nah, you know you don't.'

'Keep your hands off me, you stinking no-hoper. I ain't your partner. No way.' I pushed him away and started to leave. 'Just go, Charley, and think yourself lucky with what you have. I don't want you hanging round me, or ever crossing my path again. You and I, we're finished, savvy?'

I jerked my new hat down over my brow and wheeled away, striding across the boards to the saloon door, my spurs jingling. I had an uneasy feeling that any moment my spine might be shattered. But Charley was no back-shooter. He called me out. I'll give him that. Perhaps he really thought he could beat me.

'You lousy perfumed girly, who you think you are?' he shouted after me. 'You greasy greaser 'breed. You don't walk out on me. I'm gonna–'

I spun around, unsure whether he was going to fire or just name-call, but my Lightnings were out simultaneously and spitting lead. He had his Remington in his hand and the ball took my new hat off. But I kept firing my self-cockers until each cylinder was empty, advancing on him, pumping twelve bullets into his body. He leapt and twisted like somebody with St Vitus's dance, and, finally, hung desperately to the bar, his body pouring blood...

'Angel,' he croaked, reproachfully, shaking his head, as he hit the deck. 'I–'

148

'I think he's dead,' I said to the assembled sots. 'You all saw it. He called me out. He fired first.'

The dusky Rafaela had her arms around my waist. 'Angel, are you all right?'

'Sure.' I flashed a smile at her. 'Why?'

'I frightened for you!'

Before I could reply to that promising remark, the dumpy Pedro Borrero was pushing into the saloon.

'You again? Trouble he seem to follow you. Who he?' He nodded at the prostrate Charley.

'That pal of mine I told you about.'

'*Si?* This is how you treat your *amigos?*'

'Look, I told him we got to take the cash we got for selling the copper back to Madame Quiros. But he didn't agree. He wanted to hang on to it. When I said I'd see what you had to say about that – I was half-way to the door, my back turned – and he challenged me. What was I supposed to do? Let him shoot me down like a dog?'

Rafaela jumped to confirm that Charley had fired on me, chattering shrilly in Spanish. 'I saw it all.' Plenty of others present backed this.

'It is all very convenient, no? Now there is no other witness as to what happen to

Señor Quiros.'

'Hey, that wasn't my intention. You should have got off your fat ass and questioned him earlier.'

'And, you, Alvorado, had better be careful how you speak to me. Or it may be you will be talkin' in jail.' Borrero gave me a threatening scowl and knelt over the body, confiscating Quiros's wallet, watch and cigar case. 'So thees ees Charley Bowdler? He not such big man now.'

I was about to tell him who the property belonged to, but I realized that would not gel with my story and decided to stay quiet.

Pedro Borrero then picked up Charley's heavy Remington revolver.

'A .44 calibre, huh?' He met my eyes and I nodded. The tubby Latino sheriff sighed and stood up, stuffing it into his belt. 'So, it ees goodbye Charley.'

'Aren't you going out to take a look at the other bodies?'

'No.' He made a down-turned grimace. 'It is too far. Beyond my jurisdiction. You leave them lying on trail, you say?'

'We had to make a run for it.'

'So?' he shrugged. 'In few days buzzards have them. Sun bleach bones. Why worry? You say this cash on Bowdler belong to

150

Señora Quiros?'

'Yes, *and* that in his room.'

'And you go back to her *rancho* to return it to her?'

'Yes' – I glanced at Rafaela – 'in a few days. When I've got up the nerve to try that journey alone again. And I need to buy a good horse.'

'OK. I trust you. I release this cash to you. But I theenk enquiries will be made to see eef your word is good. I advise you not to try to disappear. You would not wish to be wanted man with price on your head?'

'No, Sheriff. I may be a *vaquero,* but I am an honest man. I like everything to be above board.'

'OK. You free to go.' He slapped my shoulder. 'But, please, while you in my town you try to stay out of trouble.'

Trouble was the last thing I wanted. Lady Fortune was smiling on me. The amiable Pedro Borrero had swallowed my lies and there was nobody to say otherwise. To double my luck, when I took a look down at the town corral I heard a bunch of men hanging over the bars talking enviously of an Arab stallion grey that was stepping back and forth around the corral. He was long-legged, delicate and graceful with a proud arch to the toss of his head, his muscles rippling beneath his coat, and his chest was very deep. He had the unmistakable lines of a thoroughbred, and, according to the men, he was descended from a line with great stamina. What's more, his Spanish owner was putting him up for auction. I outbid them all and got him for $220 in golden pesos. It was a helluva high price for a horse and I hoped he would prove his worth. I bought the Spanish saddle with its silver pommel and cantle and silver studded bridle that went with him for another sixty dollars and called him Silver. Yes, I felt like a real *caballero* once I was up and astride.

It was a lot of cash to splash out. Legally, I suppose, it was Belle's. But we were to be married in a few weeks, weren't we? So the money was as good as mine. That's how I figured it, anyhow. And, if I was going to settle down with one woman for life and vow fidelity, I might as well have one last fling, my last bachelor party, you could say.

Rafaela was in every way the opposite to Belle. It was not just that Belle was blonde, pale-skinned and more curvaceously set up, whereas Rafaela was dark and lithe. No, there was something hard and hot, something animal-like about Belle. When I was with her she magnetized me, there was no other woman. I wanted her and she wanted me. She took a lot out of a man, and, at the same time, I was never sure of her. Rafaela was more light-hearted, however, just a laughing-eyed Spanish girl, undemonstrative and easy to get on with. I could relax with her. Maybe she was mainly interested in relieving me of a good bit of my gold pesos, but I spent on her willingly. Why not, I had plenty? And I was winning at the roulette wheel, thanks to a little help from her. The week we spent together whirled by in a welter of gambling, drinking and love-making. She was as easy-going and fun to be with in bed as she was when we strolled around the town or went out riding, me on my fine thoroughbred, she on her pony. In some ways, it seemed to me, we would have made a good team. But, hell, I was committed to Belle and to being a rich ranch- and mine-owner. Once this cash had run out I would be back to being just some down-at-heel *vaquero*. And, let's face it, Rafaela was only a gambling girl and part-time prostitute.

So, I didn't say goodbye. I rose before dawn one morning, kissed Rafaela softly on the cheek as she slept, her hair tumbled on the pillow. She murmured and reached for me, but I whispered that I was going out to take a walk. I buckled on my gunbelt and left her. I walked along to the livery, saddled the tall, spirited stallion, tied my two heavy pouches of gold and silver to the cantle, slung my Winchester across my back and rode out of town as streamers of clouds were flushed scarlet and gold by the rising sun. I couldn't bear to say goodbye to Rafaela, see the tears in her dark eyes and, maybe, feel them in mine. I rode out on the journey I had been dreading; the long *Jornada del Muerto*.

Twelve

It was 4 a.m. when I left Mesilla and the settlements of Dona Ana, and for the first ten miles I put the stallion to an easy lope for I wanted to save his strength for the 125 miles between us and Socorro. A sense of foreboding had come over me as I left all white habitation and started on the trail across the waterless desert. Every five miles I swung down, loosened his double cinch a notch and trotted along beside him awhile to give him a break from carrying me. I had wrapped my tarpaulin-covered blanket-roll across my back along with my carbine and this relieved him of some more weight. Then I would let him nuzzle a handful of water from my canteen, allowing myself one swallow, and I climbed up again. The sun rose steadily in the sky until at noonday it glared down on me like a shield of red-hot brass. In those temperatures both human and horse bodies need to be water-cooled, but there would be none naturally available unless it should rain. The blue sky was as empty as the bleak terrain all about. I kept a wary eye out but there was no sign of life. On and on we went, riding and walking, in turns, and by mid-afternoon I figured we must have covered fifty-five miles of this horrendous route. With the darkness I was planning to rest a few hours before going on.

But darkness was a way off yet. And, suddenly, I saw a spiral of dust off on a rise on my right-hand side. At first I tried to tell myself that it was just a dust-devil spinning along. But, no, my dry mouth went even dryer, if that were possible, and my empty stomach tensed with fear as I realized that these were a band of Mescalero warriors, and in much larger numbers than usual. As I watched them coming out of the haze of heat and dust, I counted up to forty of them, painted for war and armed with lances and bows. There was no point trying to parley with them. These Apaches never took male prisoners. They only took scalps. I was on foot at the time, so I tightened Silver's double girths, climbed aboard and whispered to him through my dry lips, 'Come on, boy, we're in for the ride of our lives.'

There wasn't time to stay and fight. Even

if I took a stand and brought several of them down, the rest would get me in a suicidal charge. They were still well out of range of my carbine, anyhow, which is accurate at about 200 yards, and that's when the marksman and the target are standing still! By now I could hear their spine-chilling whoops. They thought they had me. They were not coming straight at me but galloping to a point in the trail lying well ahead to cut me off. 'Hyah!' I yelled in panic, spurring the horse. We had to get there before them.

Silver went like the wind as I crouched low over his flying mane. I had never felt such a surge of power in a horse. His hoofs were pounding at such speed that we were 300 yards ahead by the time the Indians reached the road. They gave howls of anger and turned after me in pursuit. It was going to be a race for life or death.

On we went for miles and miles and my spirits sank as I realized they had no intention of giving up. This was their land and a full seventy miles lay between me and the nearest chance of assistance. I eased the stallion for a bit to let him try to gain his breath. I didn't want him dying on me.

Glancing back I could see the Mescaleros

were going all out to catch me and were getting closer. I could almost see the determination on their savage, painted faces. But one advantage I had was that none of them appeared to be armed with rifle or revolver. However, as they got closer and closer they began to let loose with their bows, and arrows hissed past my ears. There was a thud in my back and I realized that an arrow had pierced my blanket-roll. Right, it was time to answer back. I drew my right-hand Lightning and turning in the saddle fired four shots in fast succession. Whether I hit any of them I'm not certain, but it had the effect of making them drop warily back out of range. Maybe they thought to wait until I had spent all my bullets.

So, it was time to show them a clean pair of heels, demonstrate what speed the Arab stallion was capable of. Without using the spurs I urged him onwards and he raced away until they were 500 yards or more behind me. I eased the pressure and again they gradually narrowed the gap until I felt, with alarm, arrows grazing my arms and thighs. So I pulled out my left-hand Lightning and glancing back glimpsed one of them roll into the dust. Again they checked their mounts and fell back out of gunshot.

For mile after mile this went on as I nursed the great strength and stamina of my horse, easing him until I felt arrows flying once more, then spurting ahead.

How long could this go on for? I wondered. The persistence of the pursuit both amazed and alarmed me. Suddenly it occurred to me it wasn't me they were after – it was my magnificent horse. Although I, of course, would be killed if they caught up, and horribly tortured if taken alive.

By 8 p.m. it was growing dark and we were still pounding along. The sky was clear, the moon rising bright. My hope that darkness might, as was customary, deter them, was to be disappointed. These boys weren't in the game of giving up. But, no, perhaps they were? We had entered a hilly section of the trail. They had been about 400 yards behind me. Suddenly they had disappeared. Or could it be they knew a short cut? Panic gripped me and for the first time I spurred Silver cruelly to his topmost speed, hanging on to him for dear life. He responded, charging along the hilly trail at full gallop for at least a quarter of an hour. Just as we reached the edge of the rough stretch the Apaches struck the road again. When they saw me still in the lead they screamed with rage and set off after me.

It was time to do something drastic if I was to stay ahead and that was to lighten my stallion's load. I had been debating this step for some while. Reluctantly, very much so, I drew my hunting knife and slashed away the heavy bags of silver and gold pesos. Apaches weren't much interested in cash – what good was it to them? – but it might make them pause to investigate.

I could sense the stallion's waning strength and we still had some hard riding to do. We had long ago passed the point where Quiros and the others had been killed and I had glimpsed their grisly corpses lying there. But that was forty miles out of Socorro. I guessed there must be before me another ten miles or so of trail to go. The only good thing was that I knew the Mescaleros must be weakening, too, and, in fact, it seemed that half their number had gradually dropped out of the chase. It was time to give them something more to think about.

By now my revolvers were empty, so I unlooped my Winchester from my back. It's no easy feat to ride with reins looped over the saddle horn, your body twisted round, aiming at a pursuer, using both hands to lever slugs into the magazine. So I waited for a straight piece of trail, eased the horse, and, as they got near, let loose a steady stream of fire. Nor is it easy to hit a moving target in such a manner but my first volley of six successive bullets knocked three Messys from their mounts.

I returned my attention to the trail for a while and, looking back, saw that the chase had thinned out some more. Now there were only half a dozen hanging on to me. I had intended to keep my loaded carbine ready in case my horse went down under me and I had to make a last stand. But now I knew I was almost to Socorro. I turned and let them have it again. Two threw up their hands and were catapulted off their broncs this time and, as the 'dobes and lights of Socorro came into view about a mile away, the rest finally hauled in. All except one.

Had I spent all twelve in the magazine? I wasn't sure. I urged the Arab on for another half-mile. But he was through galloping. I let him slow and turned to meet my lone pursuer. I was breathing hard, my heart pounding from the chase. The Mescalero was up close but he, too, slowed when he saw me waiting, and fixed an arrow in his bow. I planned to wait until he was forty yards away. It was just me and him. I reckoned I only had one bullet and I needed to make sure. I had no time to reload. At fifty yards he let his arrow fly and I reacted by instinct jerking my head aside as it hissed past my ear.

When he saw me with the carbine aimed at his heart, taking first pressure on the bullet, he pulled in. In the moonlight I could see the defiance in his gleaming eyes as he waited to die. He was just a youth, in red headband and loin-cloth, lean and dark, riding bareback, lighter than me. He had a big black bronc that was shuddering and gasping for breath, as was mine. I took first pressure on the trigger as he went to reload his bow. I was going to blast a hole through his chest, but, for some reason, I deflected my sights at the last second and my slug scorched into his right upper arm and out the other side. He dropped the bow and grasped the wound, his face a retch of pain. He wouldn't be shooting any more arrows for a while. He waited for me to finish him and perhaps he wished I would. I put up my Winchester and called to him, 'You lose this time, Apache.'

He stared at me, his lips widening in a grin. He nodded, turned his horse and walked it away, back into the darkness of Apache land.

'Come on, boy,' I said, 'we're nearly there.'

The streets of Socorro were still buzzing with life, noise and music coming from the cantinas. It was one in the morning when I cantered Silver in and slid from his spittle-flecked and sweat-streaming sides. He was heaving and gasping, unsteady, his head tossing. Another five miles and he would never have made it. I could hardly walk myself. I staggered into the saloon and leaned against the bar.

'Gimme a drink,' I croaked out, hardly able to speak.

'Tequila?'

'No, water.'

Men lounging at tables, drinking and gambling, fell silent as they stared at me. 'Look at that,' one hissed. 'He's got an arrow in his back!'

I unhitched my bedroll and sure enough there was a greasewood, flint-tipped arrow stuck in the tarpaulin, and two others caught in the folds.

'I've come seventy miles at a run,' I told them, hoarsely. 'A big gang of Messy after me. The last gave up half a mile outa town.'

I tipped a flagon of water back and nothing had ever tasted so good. More men, who had heard the shooting out on the trail in the night, came flocking in to question me.

'Seventy miles non-stop on the run,' one said. 'That ain't possible.'

'Well, that's what we did. I left Mesilla – a hundred and twenty-five miles away – at four yesterday morning. I musta killed half a dozen of 'em and they still kept coming.'

More men clustered round me and a reporter from the *Socorro Citizen* wanted to interview me.

'Gimme a keg of whiskey,' I said, slapping down one of my last remaining gold coins from my pocket.

'Whatcha goin' to do – celebrate?'

'No, I'm gonna try to save the horse that saved my hide.'

Silver was stood, his ribs still pounding, blowing and snorting his pain, his eyes glazed. He limped badly as I led him to the livery. His eyes rolled as if sensing his own fast-approaching death.

'That hoss is done fer,' a man opined.

'Not yet he ain't,' I replied. 'You don't know this horse.'

They woke the livery owner who hurried

down to open up. 'Get me some clean straw,' I shouted. 'First thing we got to do is get his shoes off. They're red hot still from galloping.'

My head was spinning and I was almost dropping on my feet myself, but I knew I had some hard work in front of me. He had saved my life and I had to save his. The next two hours, as the crowd drifted away, I spent rubbing him down with clean straw. I washed him all over with a mixture of water and whiskey, a trick my daddy had taught me. Then I rubbed him dry again.

I mixed the whiskey with two quarts of water and gave him that to drink. I had asked the town butcher to fetch me two pounds of raw steak minced fine. He thought I wanted it for myself, but I prepared a mess of cut hay sprinkled with water and stirred the steak into it. I was much relieved when Silver began to chomp his way through it.

By then five hours had passed as, left alone, I prepared a bed of deep clean straw and made the stallion lie down. I wrapped his legs and body in blankets and watched him fall asleep. Was it a sleep he would wake from? I wondered. But I had done all I could do. Funnily enough, I gave his brow a kiss like he might be a child in a cradle.

I knocked back what was left of the whiskey and went to take a room at the town hotel which was just opening. I don't remember going to sleep. I must have hit the bed and passed out. The next thing I knew was the reporter fellow shaking me awake.

'Mister, you gonna sleep for ever?'

'How long I been out?' I asked.

'Twenty-four hours.'

He showed me the *Socorro Citizen* banner headline:

MAN SURVIVES 70-MILE NON-STOP CHASE.

'Arrows in his back,' said sub-head. 'Miracle he was not killed.'

'Yeah, I guess my angel was looking after me. If one of them arrows had been one inch higher I would have been a goner.'

I filled him in on a few more details. It looked like I was the town hero. Everybody wanted to talk and buy me drinks. What made my day was that Silver was on his feet and looking just fine.

Thirteen

'Hey-ho, Silver,' I called as I rode out of Socorro mighty refreshed if, once again, with little in my pocket except loose change. The grey stallion had made a good recovery, but I could sense a change in him. There wasn't the spring in his stride that there once was. That long nightmare ride had taken a terrible toll. He would never be the horse he had been. However, we were both in good spirits to be out on the trail. I set off before nightfall planning to complete the fifty miles to the Broken Back mine by morning, but took it easy on him. It was about eight a.m. when I rode in.

'Belle!' I shouted eagerly, as I jumped up on to the porch. The front door was bolted and there was no answer to my knock, so I went round the side to the kitchen, and pushed inside.

A long-legged dude was sat at the table, dressed in a well-cut three-piece suit of expensive cloth. He had obviously just finished breakfast of ham and eggs to judge

167

by the appetizing cooking smell, and was lounging back in a rocker, his boots stuck out, sipping a cup of coffee and smoking a cheroot.

'Howdy.' His handsome face beneath fawn hair, broke into a benevolent smile as he eyed me.

I must admit I was taken aback by his presence. He seemed to have made himself at home.

'Where's Belle?'

He jerked his head towards the bedroom and, at that moment, Belle stepped from it. She was barefoot, in a skirt that exposed her calves, and a Mexican blouse. She was brushing her blonde hair back behind one ear.

'Oh, hello,' she said. 'You're back.'

'Who's he?' I asked belligerently, for there seemed to be something familiar about this cosy breakfast.

'Marshal Pat Garrett. He's not been here long.'

'You're just the man I want to see.' The United States marshal was six-foot-four, six-eight in his Stetson hat and high-heeled boots. He cut quite an impressive figure, slim, but with a deep, corncrake voice. 'I been hearing a lot about you.'

'About me – why?' I asked, nervously, helping myself to coffee from the pot.

He grinned again, showing a mouthful of teeth as strong as a horse's. In fact, he reminded me of a horse with his solid prow of a nose, the high-carved bones beneath tanned skin creased with laughter lines. His grey eyes in their slits twinkled merrily. He seemed to find life, or me, amusing.

'Why not? You've got quite a reputation.'

'Look, I don't know what all this is about but I've got some bad news for Belle,' I said, looking suitably mournful.

'Yes, she's heard. I broke it to her. I'm investigating just how Alexandre Quiros was murdered.'

'You know?' I asked Belle, and she nodded. I considered this and went on. 'I've told the Mesilla sheriff about it. It was an Apache attack. I'm sorry, Belle. There was nothing I could do to save him.'

Belle looked at me, frowned and shook her head, but I wasn't sure what she was trying to tell me. Come to think of it, I never was sure what was passing through her mind.

'Are you sure about that?' Garrett boomed in his deep voice.

'Sure, I'm sure. You want to hear what I told–?'

'Sheriff Pedro Borrero? He's already told me.'

'Told you?' I repeated like an idiot.

'Yes, I had been down to El Paso with a posse of men to bring back a wanted prisoner they were holding. We passed through Mesilla on the way back. The sheriff gave me your version of events. He told me you'd had a falling-out with your pal, Charley Bowdler, and shot him dead. He figured it was self-defence. You seemed to be having a high old time at the time' – Garrett grinned some more, and raised his eyebrows at Belle – 'so we didn't like to bother you. We rode back to Socorro and took a look at the scene of crime.'

'You did? Well, you might have taken me with you. There's safety in numbers. You should have seen what happened to me on the *Jornada del Muerto*–'

'Yeah,' he butted in. 'I've seen it. It's in the paper. You're quite the regular hero, aincha, Angel?'

'That's the truth what happened.'

'That might be the truth that happened on the way back' – Garrett stared at the ceiling and blew a smoke ring – 'but I'm interested in the truth of what happened on the way there. And, I don't think you're telling it.'

'You what? Look, what gives you the right to come here–?'

'The law of this great nation gives me the right.' Again he interrupted me. 'As a US marshal I may be based in Lincoln but I have a roving commission to investigate any crimes committed in this territory. And right now I'm looking into this one.'

'Crime?' I could hear my voice going hoarse. Maybe it was the thought of a hempen necktie, a rope around it. 'What crime?'

He stood, towering over me, and stubbed the cheroot out under his heel. 'Let's see your guns. Nice pieces,' he murmured, as I handed them over and he examined them. 'Twin .38s. You use these all the time?'

'Yeah, apart from my Winchester. But I didn't fire a shot at what you call the scene of the crime. It all happened too fast for me.'

'No, I know you didn't. At least, we didn't find any .38s in the corpses. Not a very pleasant task. The heat, the vultures, the coyotes and ants had gotten to 'em by the time we got there, if you'll forgive me saying so, Belle.'

'That's OK,' she whispered. 'I know what happens to dead bodies.'

'Yes, the stench, it passeth all under-standing. Fortunately, I persuaded one of my deputies to operate on the bodies and he dug the slugs out of 'em. While he puked his guts up in the rocks, I noted the varying calibres.'

'Like I told the sheriff, these Messys who attacked us had guns.'

'Ah, yes.' He smiled again, stuffing my revolvers in his belt. 'Just a precaution, Angel, in case you get angry. After all, I *am* doubting your veracity. So, that's how you explain the Indian lance in that somewhat obese abdomen, if I may say so, of Mr Quiros, and the arrow sticking in Shoot's chest?'

'Sure.' The guy certainly had the gift of the gab and I was going over my story hastily in my mind. I couldn't afford to make a mistake with this character. 'The Messys jumped us, killed them. Me and Charley made a run for it on the wagon.'

'Interesting, but, to me, somewhat im-plausible.' Pat Garrett grinned at me in his friendly rattlesnake fashion again. 'We made a search of the area and we found a .45 Frontier and a .32 snub-nosed Shopkeeper in the rocks. One I believe was Shoot's, the other, Mrs Quiros agrees, was her husband's. Why should the Mescaleros – if Messys, as you call them, there were – throw away valuable hardware? And why forego their usual practice of cutting their victims' hair, heart, eyes and genitals out? Again, if Belle will forgive me speaking plainly.'

'How the hell should I know? I guess they were in a hurry to get after us.'

'Yet, on a heavy wagon, through Apache-infested territory over eighty miles you made your escape from Indians who were on fast horses?'

'That's what happened.'

'Is it?' Suddenly Garrett's elbow jutted backwards into my gut, his knee came up into my groin, and he had me by my silk neckerchief, slapping his hard, horny hand across my face, before he let me fall groaning and squirming to the floor. 'Is it?' he shouted down at me.

I couldn't speak for a while, just lay there, the nausea in me, staring up at him, expecting his boots to start kicking me. I heard him apologizing to Belle for the unfortunate fracas as he glowered down at me, hauled me to my feet, slapped me hard across the jaw once more, and bellowed, 'Come on, Angel. I've had enough of this. Just give me the truth.'

'OK,' I cried, cowering away from him, still in no state to defend myself. 'Let me go. I'll tell you.'

He sat me roughly on a chair, let me calm myself, even handed me a glass of water. 'Right. Shoot.'

'It was like this,' I said, glancing at Belle as I took some water, and spat blood, feeling with my tongue at a loosened tooth. 'We had stopped to rest when Dan Coughlan got argumentative with the boss. You know the way Quiros talked, sarcastic, goading him. Dan turned and loosed a shotgun. But Quiros got him first with his little Storekeeper. He turned it on me but I said this was nothing to do with me. Shoot came up with his .45 but again Quiros was too quick – he sure moved fast. But not fast enough. Charley killed him with his .44 Remington. I didn't even draw my guns. I thought Charley was going to kill me, too. I told him those shots would attract Indians and he needed me. He agreed and concocted this stupid story about being attacked by Messys. It was him stuck the arrow and lance into their bodies. He had brought the weapons along in the wagon for this reason. Apparently, those three had it all planned beforehand. The reason was they had found

174

out that as well as copper Quiros was carrying a consignment of gold. I didn't know that. It was news to me.'

I paused and took another drink, reviewing my words, wondering what to say next. But I've always been an adept liar, so went on: 'When we got to Mesilla, Charley sold the gold to some Mexican and I reported his version of events to the sheriff. Later on, I met Charley in a saloon and told him we ought to take the gold and silver coin back to Belle. By rights it was hers. He told me I was crazy. I walked away. He called me out. I turned, going for my Lightnings. He fired. But I was faster. It's as simple as that.'

'So, what happened next?'

'I gotta admit I spent some of the gold – well, I figured I'd earned it – having a time at the tables. Then, after a few days, I set off on the *Jornada* to bring the bulk of it back to Belle.'

'You did that because you're an honest cowpoke?' he scoffed. 'And she's now your boss?'

'Of course. I *am* honest. Always have been. In fact, I was on a winning streak. Won back more than I spent. I set off and you've heard how I got chased all them miles by the 'pache.'

'Yeah, stirring stuff.'

'So, what happened to my money?' It was the first time Belle had spoken since the interrogation began, and her voice was as hard as her pale face as she stared at me.

'It was too much weight. I had to throw it away. That was in the *Citizen* wasn't it?'

'That's your story,' she said. 'How do I know you didn't stash it somewhere and are just waiting to go back and get it one day?'

'Yeah, that's a good question, Angel.'

'Because I didn't have friggin' time to. I was running for my life.'

Garrett took out my guns from his belt and placed them on the dresser. He resumed his seat in the rocker, sticking out his lanky legs and lighting another cheroot. 'Is it too early for a drink?'

'Why not?' Belle shrugged. 'What you want, Marshal, wine or whiskey?'

'Wine'll be fine.' He seemed to be in deep thought as Belle sought glasses and a bottle of Quiros's famous Chardonnay and splashed it out into three glasses. 'All the best,' he said, tossing his back in one gulp.

'So, what now?' I said.

'What now?' He got to his feet and found his hat. 'I guess I'll get back to Lincoln. Sorry I had to rough you up a bit, Angel. I

176

find it loosens men's tongues.'

He didn't say whether he believed my new story, but I assumed he must. 'So long,' he drawled, gave us his crocodile smile, and swung outside.

We watched him mount his horse and ride away, straight-backed and confident, singing some song. I put my arm around Belle's waist.

'Phew! That was a close one. That man is not nice to know.' I turned to kiss her and she succumbed, licking at the blood on my lips, but then she pressed me away.

'No, Angel, this is no good. We must wait. You must go out on the range, act like one of the hands. That man will be watching us like a hawk.'

'Aw, come on. I've had a helluva ride.'

'No, I mean it, Angel. You've done well. We'll stick to your story that it was the other three. But, you and I, we've got to stay away from each other for a bit. I'm the grieving widow, for Chrissakes. And that man, he's on to us. I know that.'

'He can't prove anything.' I tried to pull her into me, but she backed away. 'Come on, Belle. I done this for you. I need you.'

'No!' she shrilled. 'We've got to do it right, Angel. A brief period of mourning and then

... you know ... maybe...'

'Aw, please yourself,' I shouted, slamming the door as I went out to see to the horse.

Fourteen

From being a smouldering, sensuous siren Belle Quiros suddenly became as cold as an iceberg towards me. When I came in from tending her cattle out on the range she would not let me into the ranch house. She even barred and shuttered the windows so I couldn't make a forcible entry. Whenever I did get near enough to manhandle her she fended me off, threatened to scream for help. Our hot passion was a thing of the past and when a woman puts up a cold front there's not much a man can do to melt her except play along.

'What's the matter, *amigo?*' Jesus Guttierez seemed to find it amusing as I kicked my heels in the bunkhouse. 'She kick you out now she the boss lady?'

'What about that seam of gold?' I had gone down the shaft to take a look one day at the miners, in a gloomy cavern lit by carbide lamps, hacking at the walls. 'How big is it? How long will it last?'

'It big enough, but I no say. Señor Quiros

he tell me to keep mouth shut.' Jesus waved a warning finger at me. 'The lady say so, too. I speak word it curtains for me. So, I know nothing.'

'You mean she'd fire you, or kill you?'

Jesus shrugged. 'I dunno. I just do what she tell me.'

Well, I was no miner, and knew nothing, myself, on the subject. My cursory examination of the sparkling seam of ore meant little to me, but I guessed by the amount they were bringing out there would soon be enough for another wagon-load. I did not relish another trip along the *Jornada del Muerto*, but it crossed my mind that if I did go it might be as well to get what I could, this time, and get out.

Belle was playing hot and cold. Of course, she could not avoid me all the time and once when we did meet out by the corral she hissed at me, 'Be patient, Angel. It's going to take time to sort out his affairs, to get his capital together. In two or three months' time, when I'm ready, we'll be together, I promise.'

'You'll marry me?'

'Yes.' She stared at me with those hazy, speckled eyes of amber and green that I could never fathom. 'Why not?'

The sour-faced Harry, in his black clothes, black hat, shotgun crooked over his arm, was never far away when she stepped out, and at that time he was sitting on the house porch, watching us, but out of earshot.

'He's threatened me,' she said. 'He knows all about us. He says he's sure we planned Alexandre's death between us. He's gonna go to the marshal and tell him everything unless I pay him a thousand dollars within a week.'

'Well,' I sighed. 'He's blackmailing the right person. It ain't no good him asking me 'cause I'm broke.'

'You've got to kill him,' she said. 'If he spills what he knows to Pat Garrett we'll both hang.'

'Kill him? Are you joking? So that's why you're sweetening me? I thought there must be something to it. No, count me out, Belle. I've had enough of killing.'

'You've got to, Angel. You want to marry me, don't you? You want all this? With him out of the way we would be free.'

'Change the subject,' I replied. 'He's coming over. I'll think about it.'

The unsavoury Harry crunched across the yard and gave us a baleful glower, his eyes shaded by his hatbrim.

'Anythan you need me for, Miz Quiros?'

Belle bridled, haughtily. 'No, thank you.'

'Now your pals Shoot, Dan and Charley are all dead you gonna be needing more hands to help with the stock, aincha, Angel?' he growled. 'Maybe we should take a trip into White Oaks, an' at the same time you could attend to that li'l arrangement we spoke about, Belle.'

Belle took a deep breath and stared pleadingly at me.

'Very well, we'll do that.' She turned on her heel with a swish of her skirts and went back to the house.

Shotgun Harry watched her go and grinned his tobacco-stained teeth. 'Just in case she been givin' you instructions to put a bullet in my back I better warn you I've writ down everything I know about you two. I've lodged the letter in the bank at Lincoln with instructions that if anything happens to me it's to be handed over to the US marshal straight away. Savvy?'

I took this surprise information in and nodded. 'Sure, I savvy. You got us hogtied, in other words.'

'You could say that,' Harry grinned, before sauntering away.

Belle certainly looked the part of the

mourning widow when we set off two days later in the early dawn for the long ride into White Oaks, she beside me on the box of the buggy, Harry riding alongside. Her hair was drawn back into a severe bun beneath her black hat and veil, her lips were unpainted and as pale as her powdered face which had no trace of rouge, and she wore an ankle-length black dress of satin with high-buttoned bootees.

There had been another storm and black rainclouds went rolling across the sky, the mountain peaks protruding through their low-lying haze. I could sense Belle's mood was as stormy as the weather and she was silent most of the way. When we arrived mid-afternoon I helped her step down. She quickly discarded my hand and walked through the puddles and horse-traffic across to the bank. While she was in there I busied myself buying grain, flour, dried fruit and other supplies she had jotted down on a shopping list. Sometimes I didn't feel like her ranch foreman and prospective husband – more like her errand boy and hired killer.

In the Claremont saloon Harry was sitting in a card game. I chose a table where I could sit with my back to the wall and my eye on the door in the light of past experience in this place. I propped my Winchester nearby and loosened my Lightnings, taking first bite into a bottle of tequila. When the men at the tables saw Belle arrive in her widow's weeds they dropped quiet for moments, nudging each other. She spotted me and came over.

'What you havin'?'

'Tequila's fine.' Her satin dress rustled as she settled herself, going through a bag that appeared to be stuffed with deeds and documents. 'What a business it is sorting everything out and transferring it to my name.'

'So,' I asked, 'are you a wealthy widow?'

She shrugged and took a shot, giving a grimace of her lips. 'That's my business. What are you going to do about *him?*'

'What can I do? I've told you what he said.'

'You could break in the bank at Lincoln, find that letter.'

'You really are crazy.'

'If you used a little initiative it might not be impossible. Otherwise, none of this' – she indicated the bag – 'is going to be any good to you or me.'

Harry had seen her come in. He slapped some fellow on the back and moved out of the game, pushing through the crowd, his shotgun in his hand.

'Howdy.' He sat down before us. 'You got what we agreed?'

Belle dipped in the bag and produced an envelope. 'Here. It's the first and the last you're going to get, you'd better believe that.'

Harry snatched it and peered inside, running a thumb through the wad of a thousand dollars. 'Good.' He tucked it in his suit's inside pocket. 'Glad you two lovebirds see sense. But, it ain't no use you saying that, Belle, 'cause I'm gonna expect one like this every month from here on. You better make damn sure it's here on time or the marshal's gonna be gettin' some interesting information in his ear.'

'Go to hell,' she snapped.

'Talk of the devil,' I said. 'Look who's here.'

Marshal Pat Garrett had pushed through the batwing doors, his lanky figure elegantly attired, as ever, in a suit of grey worsted, a thin gold watch chain strung across the front of his cross-over waistcoat, a celluloid collar and tie around his throat. He stood tall above the others' heads in a high-crowned Stetson and his high-heeled blood-

185

red boots. He ambled across to the bar followed by the portly Sheriff Beaver Smith, a far scruffier individual. A bottle of whiskey was put before them and Garrett poured them tumblersful.

He glanced around the saloon, carefully casing the joint for trouble or riff-raff and, when he saw us in our corner, his face split into his beaming grin and he raised the bottle to us. From the bulge under his jacket I assumed he was carrying a shoulder-hung revolver.

Belle ignored him. Her eyes through the veil were steadied on Harry. 'I'm telling you that's the last payment you can expect from me. I don't give a damn what you say. You can't prove anything.'

'Can't I?' Harry purred, tugging at his moustache. 'Who you tryin' to kid?'

'Anyway,' she protested, 'I'm not a wealthy woman. Alexandre had badly overreached himself. Most of what he had is tied up in stocks. You can't squeeze me for what I don't have.'

'Can't I?' he repeated. 'So, why don't you sell the mine and the ranch? Whatever, I'm gonna need my pocket-money on time and half of the next gold consignment you send.'

'For Christ's sake, don't go saying that

word here,' she hissed. 'We'll have half the population of White Oaks stampeding up there.'

'Fair enough. I'll stay silent on both counts. But you got plenty and I want my share.' He got up and glowered at us. 'You remember that.'

'Don't bother coming back to the ranch,' Belle said. 'I don't need you any more.'

'Oh, I'm coming back. I gotta keep an eye on you two.'

We watched him shuffle away, watched him stop to have words with the marshal, who grinned and shook his hand, before Harry sauntered out of the saloon, no doubt to start drinking his profits away in other establishments.

Garrett caught us watching and, his hip-hugging pants tight around his long shanks, he strolled over to us, glass in hand, taking off his hat. 'Howdy, boys and girls,' he said amiably, and sprawled out on the vacated chair. He lit a cigar, his teeth gleaming as he gripped it in them, and peered across. 'That is you behind that veil, ain't it, Belle?'

'Very amusing, Marshal. How can I help you?'

'Just paying my respects, ma'am,' he grinned. 'What brings you to town?'

'I'm trying to sort out my husband's tangled affairs. There is an awful lot to do.'

'Indeed, a sad duty. How ya coping? You gonna stay on and run the ranch?'

'No, I think I'll let that side of things run down. It's too much for one woman. So you needn't bother rustling up any more hands, Angel.'

'Of course, you lost the others. Premature deaths. Very unfortunate, wasn't it? Wouldn't you agree?'

'Of course.' She permitted herself to smile. 'It's no use playing cat and mouse games, Marshal. Angel's told you all he knows.'

'Has he?' Garrett stuck out his long legs and blew cigar smoke into the air, holding his long fingers out, expressively. 'Now that's what I wonder about. And, are you two, how do you say, a fixture now?'

'Of course not. I've made Angel my ramrodder, that's all.'

'Have you now?' Garrett smiled insolently at her. 'Lucky him.'

'I've booked myself a room here, by the way, Angel,' she said. 'Perhaps you can find yourself some less expensive place to stay in town. I know thirty a month don't go far. So, here's five. That should cover a meal and bed. I think I'll go up now to freshen up. See you in the morning.'

I was so taken aback by her ladylike airs, the way she tossed me the five-dollar bill, I could hardly speak. The cheek of the woman! 'Sure, don't worry about me,' I said, as she stood to leave.

Garrett stood up and bowed in over emphasized gallantry, taking her hand to squeeze. 'Belle, if it's not too soon after your husband's demise, might I invite you to dine with me?'

'Why not?' she shrugged. 'I'm going to dine here, anyway. Only I hope you won't talk shop.'

'No way.' He gave a booming laugh and relinquished her hand. 'We'll talk about the old days in Louisiana.'

He watched her ascend the hotel stairs to the landing, turned and winked at me. 'We knew each other out there,' he said, turning and strolling back to the bar.

Knew each other? What was going on here?

I spent the five dollars she had handed out to me like I was some lackey, spent it on booze. By mid-evening a fiery fury was burning in me, a self-pitying jealousy, and I was ready to breeze into the Claremont saloon and shoot that long-legged twister down. But when I stepped inside I saw him standing over the roulette table as if he hadn't a care in the world. Shotgun Harry had returned and was chucking his cash away on the whirl of the wheel as if it grew on trees.

'You're mighty plumb, aincha, Harry?' I heard Garrett drawl as I propped myself, somewhat unsteadily, at the bar.

'Aw, there's plenty more where this come from,' Harry said, grinning widely as he put his arms around a couple of avaricious whores. They were young and pretty, too, and smiled at the marshal. 'I ain't short of a dollar or two, am I, girls?'

We watched them carry the last of the big spenders upstairs, as Garrett picked up his rifle, which he had leant against the bar. 'Well, boys, I gotta be gittin' back to Lincoln. It's best to travel in darkness. See y'all.'

As he strolled out he glanced my way. 'So long, Angel. We'll meet again.'

Fifteen

'Know him? How should I know him?' Belle protested, as we drove back to the Broken Back mine. 'He knew Alexandre, apparently. Pat Garrett's family had a plantation not far from his in Louisiana. They both lost their land and their slaves after the war.'

'He told you this at dinner last night? So, why should he say you were old friends?'

'He was trying to stir you up for God's sake! He and *Alex* were friends. I used to deal blackjack on the *Memphis Queen*. I mighta met him then. I seem to remember him; he's not a man you can miss.'

'Yes,' I said enviously. 'He's got style.'

'He told me that when he came West he worked as a buffalo-hunter for a while.'

'Him? One of that foul smelly breed?'

'He did it to make money. He said he shot a hundred beasts at a single stand. He skinned them, sold the robes for five dollars each.'

'And left the carcasses rotting on the plains. What a way to earn a buck.'

191

'Work it out, Angel, five by one hundred, what's that add up to? A day? And if you're out there four or five weeks? Anyway, he told me last night he had a couple thousand dollars in his poke when he packed it in and came to New Mexico.'

Garrett was a man of my own age, hitting thirty, but I couldn't help wondering how he had got himself elected marshal.

'Look, Angel, I don't think you understand, money is what counts in this world. Without that you're nothin'. You're just trash. Pat more or less admitted to me that he slipped some clerk in the governor's office a bribe. All he did was cross out the name of the man who had been elected and put Garrett's name in instead.'

'Shee-it! You can't help admiring the guy. He's learned his lessons in the school of hard knocks. He's some character.'

'You could say that. He told me the governor, Lew Wallace, is a complete nit-wit. He's written some book, *Ben Hur*, which has sold worldwide, and all he's interested in is scribbling another success. Everybody's complaining about the violence, the lawlessness, the rustling and feuding in New Mexico, so he's given Garrett *carte blanche* to stamp it out. He's a hard man. Maybe he can do it.'

192

'Yeah, he sees people like buffaloes. Blow 'em out!'

'Don't worry, Angel. He's not worried about us. We're just small fry. There's the Lincoln county war going on, some kid, William Bonney, he's murdered more than twenty men including Sheriff Brady. He's after him.'

'Billy? – The Kid? – he'll never catch him.'

In fact, I underestimated Garrett's ruthlessness. He became notorious, less than a year later, as the killer of the Kid. He hid in a darkened room at Fort Sumner and when the Kid called out, 'Who's there? – *Quien es?*' – he shot him down. He gave him no chance. That was the kind of man we were up against.

My head was aching from the tequila as the buckboard bounced. But I guess Shotgun Harry, as he followed us along, felt worse.

I was wound up like a spring from two days of sitting beside Belle, her warmth, her scent, her hypnotic magic beside me, and being unable to touch her. When we got back to the Broken Back I got rid of Harry, and helped her carry the groceries in. Before she had even lit a hurricane lamp I grabbed her, pushing her back across the kitchen table, snatching her dress up in a desperate and urgent need. She screamed, but I had her. But, instead of responding she just went dead. She just lay there, loose-limbed, her eyes staring at the ceiling in the moonlight. It was like trying to make love to a corpse, or a dead fish. I gave up before I was through.

'Hech! Thanks very much, Belle.' I walked out and stared up at the moon. 'I've had enough of this. I know when I ain't wanted.' I saddled Silver and jumped on his back. As I rode out I heard Belle shrill, 'Angel, come back!'

Who the hell did she think she was ordering about? I rode all night across the mountains and trotted into Socorro in the morning. There everybody was glad to see me. I was a celebrity, the man who had made that amazing ride. And his horse. Folks gathered round, wanting to fondle Silver, talk to me, buy me drinks.

Well, after being patted on the back, dragged from bar to bar, given food and tequila, imagine my surprise when I felt a hard, muscle-knotted arm around my throat.

'Aiiee! Angel! I found you.'

'Rafaela!' In her flame dress, somewhat

194

sun-faded and torn, her lithe dark limbs, her tangle of black, shimmering curls, she looked more like some kind of cannibal from a desert isle. 'What you doin' here?'

'I come up with bull-team from Socorro. I look for you, Angel.'

Needless to say we ended up in bed in a room in the town hotel, the same bed I had once slept in with Belle.

'Where you been to, Angel?' she murmured after our passion was exhausted.

'I got to be straight with you, Rafaela. I been mixed up with another woman. She's got money and property. She's twisted me round her finger, got me to do thing I never oughta done. But it's gone sour. She ain't gonna marry me. And I don't want her no more, anyway. I want you, *chiquita*.'

'Ah, Angel, if only we could,' she whispered. 'If we would be married I would be the happiest girl alive.'

'Yeah, maybe, but we wouldn't be happy without money. Look, Rafaela, I'm gonna go back. She wants me to drive another wagon-load of copper and gold down the *Jornada*. I'll recruit five or six men so we're well protected. You'll come along. I'll sell the gold in Mesilla. And, then, you and me, we'll head for Old Mexico. We'll be rich and we'll be free. How say you?'

For reply, she gripped me around the neck with her skinny arms and showered me with kisses, jumping on top of me. 'Git sat on, gal,' I said. 'We're goin' for another ride.'

It was strange. Whereas Belle was voluptuous, warm as milk, creamy white and soft, and hard-hearted, Rafaela was rough, dark, lithely muscled, slim-breasted, and yielding. She was great!

Great, that was, until the door was kicked open and Belle stood there in her dark dress, a Colt revolver in her hands and its deathly hole pointed at us. Rafaela screamed and I ducked under the sheet as the bullet crashed out, taking my new black Stetson from my head. I rolled out as more bullets smashed into the adobe wall, and, naked, wrestled her for the gun. By the time I had twisted it from her wrist it was empty and she was sobbing in my arms.

'You bastard, you *vaquero*. You are all the same. This is what you do behind my back. I want to kill you.'

I hugged her in my arms, soothing her, and raised my eyebrows at the pop-eyed Rafaela, mouthing silently to her, *'Domingo.'* And pointing, 'You, me, *vamos.'*

It took some time to soothe Belle down,

196

and get dressed, as Rafaela took the hint and disappeared, clutching her clothes. 'Aw, she's just a whore,' I said. 'You're the only one for me. Jeez, look what you done to my hat!'

This made her laugh which was strange, because then I had to make love to Belle in the same bed. When I finally buckled on my gunbelt and staggered downstairs Rafaela hooked her brown arm around my neck and pulled me into the bar.

'What you do?' she pleaded.

'It's OK,' I whispered. 'She's the rich woman. I don't want her, I want you. There's a consignment of her gold ready to roll. I'll be here on Sunday, sweetheart. Be ready to join me.'

There was only one thing that bothered me as I drove Belle back to the mine in her buggy, travelling overnight, once more, Silver trotting behind, and that was that letter Shotgun Harry had left in his bank. What should I do about that?

Lincoln is unlike most first-generation frontier communities where the houses and stores are huddled together side by side. No, it is spaciously set out on each side of a wide trail, the houses, mainly pitch-roofed and timber-built, stand on their patches of land a good way apart from each other. And this suited my purpose.

It was three a.m. when I rode in from the north. It had taken me about two days to get there from the Broken Back ranch. Two days back and the wagon of gold and copper would be ready to drive to Socorro. I should get there on the Saturday. On the Sunday, if all went to plan, I would move out along the *Jornada* with Rafaela and an armed escort. But, first I had to break into the Lincoln bank.

The first house you come to from the north is the sheriff's office and, across the dirt trail, the jailhouse. I naturally gave these a wide berth in case anyone should hear me ride in, and rode along the bank of the Rio Bonito. The moon was high so I had no difficulty picking my way. I rode up behind the big McCarthy Emporium which is in the centre of the township.

Beside it was the squat, square, adobe town bank, its windows heavily barred, its solid oak door locked. My heart, as they say, was in my mouth, because I only had a hazy idea how I was going to manage this. I had been in the bank in daylight and noticed it was in two rooms, the front one was where the customers were served, and the back one was the manager's office. Between the two was a wide chimney where in winter a log fire was lit.

I drew Silver in and loose-hitched him to a rock a short way off. I took my lariat and stealthily approached. It was easy enough to send it spinning over the chimney stack and haul myself up. I dropped the rope down, climbed in and lowered myself. It was a tight fit, but I'm pretty slim and squeezed down. What the hell would happen, it occurred to me, if I got stuck? But I landed in the hearth, half-choking on soot and the remains of a large bird's nest. I found a lantern, lit it, and went into the banker's office. There was a big solid safe with one of these recently patented locks by Yale and Son, a clever device that held a door solid as a rock.

'Hell,' I growled, for there was no way of opening that unless I used a stick of the mine dynamite I'd brought in my saddle-bag, another handy recent invention.

But I spotted a steel filing cabinet. That, too, was locked. Each of the four drawers had its contents indicated by letters of the alphabet. Shotgun Harry's surname was Roberts so maybe it would be in the N–T drawer? I pulled out my knife, a solid Bowie, and hammered it with my revolver butt at a corner of the drawer. You can guess it made quite a clanging sound so I tried to muffle it with my neckerchief. Yes, my efforts were rewarded, the drawer swung open. Breathing hard, I listened. All was silent. Holding the lantern I examined the contents. The banker was a tidy man. There it was: Roberts, Harry, on a cardboard file. Inside was a letter. I tore open the envelope and studied the contents. In an inky scrawl Harry accused me and Belle of initiating the murder plot of Quiros and added some damning evidence.

Good, I muttered as I put a match to it and let the ash flutter to the floor. Now, all I gotta do is make Harry draw on me and put him down, then I'll be free.

There was another of the Yale locks on the door, but that meant it could be opened by hand from the inside. I smiled with delight and satisfaction as I eased it ajar and stepped out into the night. Nuthin' to it!

I bent to brush some soot from my pants, and it was a good job I did, because at that second a slug smashed into the door right where my head had been. Gunfire crashed out all around me, whining and chipping the door and 'dobe. There was nothing I could do but dive back into the bank. I crawled to the window, Lightnings in both hands, and made sustained reply, firing at the flashes of explosions until my cylinders were empty.

When I leaned my back against the wall to reload I heard Pat Garrett's mocking voice call out: 'It ain't no use, Angel. We can wait even if we starve you out. We got you surrounded. Toss your revolvers through the window and come out with your hands high. I'll go easy on you.'

He was shouting to me from behind a rock corral wall on the other side of the trail and I saw the shadowy shape of his tall figure. He ducked down as I let loose a volley of lead. Then it was my turn to duck as bullets whistled through the bars, ricocheting scarily about me, pocking the walls. How many slugs had I left? About a dozen in my belt. Aw, hell!

I waited a while, wondering how they had been ready for me. Then I chucked my Lightnings out and yelled, 'Don't shoot! I'm coming out.'

Marshal Garrett strode forward, his big horse-grin on his face, and locked irons around my wrists. 'Too bad, Angel. I'm charging you with the murder of Alexandre

Quiros and attempted bank robbery, OK?'

'You know I didn't shoot him.'

'No, but you sure as hell got Charley Bowdler to. Your finger might just as well have pulled the trigger. The motive's clear, you wanted Belle and her money.'

'Yeah, an' I can prove it.' Shotgun Harry had clambered over the wall and his surly face was up close. 'I heard and saw plenty and I'll see you swing.'

At that, I smashed my clenched, manacled fists into his ugly mug and he fell back, gasping. It didn't do my case much good, but it gave me some satisfaction to see his bloody nose as they led me away to the jailhouse.

What more can I say? At the trial neither Garrett nor Roberts mentioned Belle's part in instigating our plot. Maybe they had been bribed, maybe not. The innocent, hard-done-by widow hardly glanced at me as the circuit judge banged his gavel and droned, 'I sentence you to be put to death by hanging.'

'But she – she was in on it,' I stuttered out, pointing her way.

'That is patently absurd, your honour,' Garrett remarked as I was led away in chains.

Outside the courthouse he came across to me, grinned and stuck a cheroot between my lips, lighting it for me.

'Bad luck, Angel,' he drawled. 'Somebody had to be the fall guy. And we chose you. You might be glad to hear, Shotgun Roberts may well meet with an unfortunate accident sometime soon.' He grinned again and slapped my shoulder. 'Don't worry, I'll take good care of Belle and her mine. We're planning on gittin' hitched next week. Too bad you cain't come to the ceremony.'

He left me with two burly deputies, strode over to Belle and handed her into the buggy, jumping up to take the reins himself. As they drove off Belle gave me a cold, false smile and a wave of her hand. It ain't no use my cursing her. I believe, in a way, she truly loved me, even if she betrayed me. I'm writing down this account of what happened before they hang me, just so somebody might know the truth. I can hear them hammering the scaffold into shape outside my cell window. They say I'll draw a good crowd. Ah, well, the story's ended now. And so is my journey.

Signed, Angel Alvorado,
September 3, 1880
Lincoln, New Mexico

Post Script: The above was meant to be what you might call my last will and testament. I was ready for the end. But the night before my hanging little Jesus Guttierez turned up to visit me. Marshal Garrett had gone off with Belle to get married in Last Vegas; this was to be followed by their honeymoon as I believe he wished to shield her tender susceptibilities from the sight of me swinging from a rope. He had left strict instructions to his deputies to watch me like hawks.

They frisked Jesus but never suspected he had a stick of dynamite shoved up a part of his anatomy that I'll refrain from mentioning. He passed it on to me. He also confessed that for two years he had been smuggling nuggets of pure gold out of Quiros's mine in the same hiding place and had a stash of it which he planned to take down the *Joranda del Muerto* while Belle was away. However, he said he needed a fast gun like me for protection.

'Boom!' The dynamite did its trick, blowing out the barred window of the adobe cell. Jesus had my stallion, Silver, waiting not far away as I leaped out through the dust, and he had broken into the marshal's office to

204

retrieve my Lightnings. A succession of well-placed shots to legs and arms deterred the deputies from following.

When we reached the Broken Back ranch Jesus called to Shotgun Harry and, as he stepped out of his cabin, I was on the roof and neatly caught him in my noose, stringing him high. I was tempted to leave him to kick his last, but cut him down and hogtied him, as he had once tried to hogtie me.

'*Adios*, Harry,' I called, as we set off with a wagon-load of gold ore to collect Jesus's bonus of pure nuggets. I was a week late for my date with Rafaela but she was waiting and ready to go.

I now have to confess that I did not tell Belle or the marshal the truth about those two bags of gold and silver pesos I was carrying when I fled from the Mescaleros. I slowed and tossed them into a hole in the rocks. A peculiarly shaped cactus marked the spot and we retrieved them on the way down to Mesilla. Soon we were across the border to safety.

Surprisingly, I have stayed remarkably out of trouble since then. Me and Rafaela have raised a brood of kids on our hacienda in Old Mexico, while Jesus and his wife have done much the same. Maybe our stolen gold wasn't necessary to our happiness, but in this land where most others live in grinding poverty, it certainly helped. We have to keep our guns well oiled because the land is infested by bandits. But the biggest bandit of all is el Presidente Diaz in his palace in Mexico City. There is much talk of revolution so I am covering my bets both ways by paying lip-service to Diaz and giving shelter to a swarthy madman called Pancho Villa, who plans to turn the country on its head.

Oddly enough, I heard that Shotgun Harry was assassinated, shot in the back, when he stepped down from his horse at some lonesome spot to urinate by the side of the trail. I never saw Belle or Pat Garrett again but Garrett eventually suffered an identical fate. Who, I wonder, could have been the hired gunman? Nobody seems to know. They both had plenty of enemies. And, as they say in Mexico, only death ends a feud. And we all have our own *Jornada del Muerto* to undergo.

The publishers hope that this book has given you enjoyable reading. Large Print Books are especially designed to be as easy to see and hold as possible. If you wish a complete list of our books please ask at your local library or write directly to:

Dales Large Print Books
Magna House, Long Preston,
Skipton, North Yorkshire.
BD23 4ND

This Large Print Book, for people
who cannot read normal print,
is published under the auspices of

THE ULVERSCROFT FOUNDATION